HERMINE
AN ANIMAL LIFE

A NOVEL BY
MARIA BEIG

TRANSLATED FROM THE GERMAN BY
JAIMY GORDON

New Issues Poetry & Prose

Western Michigan University
Kalamazoo, Michigan 49008

First published in Germany © 1984 by Jan Thorbecke Verlag
GmbH & Co., Sigmaringen.
English translation © 2004 by Jaimy Gordon.

An Inland Seas Book

 Inland Seas Books are supported by a grant from
The Michigan Council for Arts and Cultural Affairs.

Copyright © 2005 by Maria Beig. All rights reserved.
Printed in the United States of America.

First American Paperbound Edition, 2005.

ISBN: 1930974485 (paperbound)

Library of Congress Cataloging-in-Publication Data:
Beig, Maria
Hermine: an animal life/Maria Beig
Library of Congress Control Number: 2004101974

Editor:	Jonathan Pugh
Art Director:	Tricia Hennessy
Designer:	Carly Queen
Production Manager:	Paul Sizer
	The Design Center
	Department of Art
	College of Fine Arts
	Western Michigan University

This book is a work of fiction. Names, characters, places and incidents either are products of the author's imagination or are used fictiously. Any resemblance to actual events or locales or persons, living or dead, is entirely coincidental.

HERMINE
AN ANIMAL LIFE

**A NOVEL BY
MARIA BEIG**

**TRANSLATED FROM THE GERMAN BY
JAIMY GORDON**

WESTERN MICHIGAN UNIVERSITY

The translator is deeply indebted to Peter Blickle
for lending his wisdom to every page of this book.

Contents

Translator's note	3
Introduction	9
Child	11
Girl	75
Miss	97
Wife	137
Change	171

Translator's note

Maria Beig was born in 1920, one of thirteen children of a farm family, in rural Swabia, a few miles from Lake Constance, on Germany's southern border. The sensitive, observant child was not handy around the farm, nor did her marital prospects look good (there were six brothers and sisters in line before her), so she was given an education. She attended *Frauenarbeitsschule* ("school for women's work") during the thirties and began teaching home economics and handicrafts in public schools in early wartime. A good deal later she married, in her mid-thirties. She has one daughter.

Beig did not write until she was nearly sixty. A disabling depression caused her to retire early from teaching. She took up painting, then playing the flute. Nothing helped until she began to write. She had finished three handwritten, block-lettered manuscripts before she was invited to read at a forum for local writers where her future publisher happened to be in the audience.

Beig's first two novels in print, *Raven's Croak* (1982) and *Lost Weddings* (1983), caused a sensation with their grim depictions of Catholic farm and village life in southern Germany, and especially of women's experience of this life, brutal and thankless. Her stark realism and unornamented, laconic style encouraged readers and reviewers to look for the sources of Beig's stories in her own life. As a result, the brother who had inherited the family property forbade Beig not only his house but even the small village where she had grown up. At a reading in nearby Ravensburg, Beig was interrupted repeatedly by cries from the audience: "Liar!" and *"Nestbeschmutzer!"*—soiler of the nest. She gave up public readings, but not writing books. In

2002, at the age of 81, she published her twelfth volume.

Plainly, when Maria Beig became, more or less overnight, at the age of sixty-two, a famous, even a notorious, writer in Germany, she was unacquainted with any literary establishment. Nor had German critics ever heard of Maria Beig, who had grown up on a farm and spent some thirty-five years teaching knitting in provincial schools before she began to write. Critics preferred, at first, to explain to themselves the undeniable power of her work—its remarkable economy and aura of grim authenticity—as the power of the primitive, the raw, the untaught. Even novelist Martin Walser, who championed her work from the start, praised her in these terms:

> As for its literary value—Maria Beig's writing seems to me something that grew in the field, whereas all the rest of us writers had to grow in the garden. The difference is as between garden sage and meadowsage, in fragrance and fire.

But Beig's third published novel, *Hermine: An Animal Life*—her most autobiographical book, and in fact the first book she wrote—anticipated in both form and substance some of the most sophisticated fictive innovations of our day. It is the most unconventional of her books, her own favorite among them, as well as the one that has made the deepest impression upon other writers because of the striking originality of its structure.

The story of a woman but also a bestiary, it is a life told in sixty-four animals. Thus Beig presents a human life as so many variations, or discrete narrative takes, on a single obsession. Her protagonist, Hermine, is in some sense each of the animals she encounters in the sixty-four chapters of the book, all of which are brief: the average length is less than two pages. In composing a book-length text out of "short short" fictions—many less than a page long—each of which has a claim to be able to stand alone, Beig was before her time in 1984, and still is: twenty years later, the literary vogue of the "short short" has not arrived in Germany, although Beig, in *Hermine,* proves herself to be one of its most inventive practitioners.

Many an author nowadays tries to use sequence, as opposed to continuous narrative, as an organizing principle: Beig is one of the few writers to have created a whole novel (if *novel* is not too regressive—or too modern—a word for *Hermine)* with this design. In stressing sequence and repetition over chronological development, Beig creates an aesthetic symmetry that is at once comforting (pattern is strongly discernible) and disturbing (the pattern does not add up to meaning in any usual sense). Even her reaching behind the conventions of the novel towards a form as antique, as encyclopedic, and as fundamentally imaginary, as the medieval bestiary, is a supremely postmodern gesture. Granted, like all truly successful experimenters with narrative, Beig manages, slyly, to tell a story in the end, and even incorporates chronology—*Child, Girl, Miss, Wife, Change* are the five parts of her book—into her sequence.

Above all, Maria Beig is ahead of her time in her reevaluation of the position of the human on the ladder of being. In *Hermine,* human and animal life are not safely separated. From the outset, the heroine of the book leads the life of an animal among animals. As one of a great flock of children, as one of the animals of the farm, she is assessed in value by the owners according to her physicality (puny), her practical usefulness (slight), even her dung (wormy). Among farm animals, she comes out at the bottom, for she can't impose her will even on the dumb creatures of the barnyard. Quite the opposite: the thick-skinned, thick-witted animals dominate her too. Her nerve is not suited to the grim work of the farm; the other animals are better adapted than she to their natures and fates. Since against this background all her uniqueness is negative uniqueness, for Hermine the safest course is to be as much like the other animals as possible. And herein lies the paradox: Finally the life of the heroine of *Hermine* is singular enough to be the basis for fiction not because it is an extraordinary life but because it knows itself to be indistinguishable from the lives of the other animals. That is where her interest for Maria Beig lies.

Well-adapted or not, animals must suffer in *Hermine:* They die, become crippled, are slaughtered, shot or eaten by other animals. We sense that their fates mirror Hermine's inner defeats. A good many animals in the book are oddly drawn to the heroine: seeming to see through her weakness, they menace that boundary between human and animal that would safely separate them if only she were able to assert the proper mastery. In the very last chapters of *Hermine,* the sense of shame she has carried with her all her life for being subject to animals in this way is transfigured into the clearsightedness it has, in fact, been all along. Only one who has known, in the flesh, this equality of being between human and animal, can traverse the boundary in the other direction: Now she sees, she feels; she is privileged, rather than condemned, to cross over; in the best sense, she is one of them.

—Jaimy Gordon
Kalamazoo, February 2004

Introduction

This is about a human life. Not that this person is anything special. What is strange about her is only the animals; because of them her story will be told. They aren't even rare animals, as you might suppose. Except for one from a foreign land, they're just the usual for the country. Plenty of times the same animal turns up, or anyway ones of the same species, so that, sad to say, you won't get much of a lesson in animals out of the story either.

Like a red thread, no, like bumps of thick brown cord, encounters with animals weave through her life. Towards the end it's true the cord turns into a silken thread, so that to keep from losing track, you could wind up the coil from that end. But since it's as if some kind of thread was there from the start, it shall be unwound from its beginning.

Her name will be Hermine, for even when she was small she wished she had that name. She grew up in a time when you heard a lot about *hehre* maidens, maids of noble mien. The *her* of the beautiful name struck her as proud and lordly, the *mine* she understood as diligent and kind. And that's how she wanted to be. Naturally she didn't get this magnificent name, but another one quite ordinary. Every household had one of those.

Child

Horse

It shied at a foreign curse and raced downhill. The harness swung around behind it and struck mother's three-year-old dead. Now, no human being warrants such hopes as a three-year-old. Then you marvel at its intelligence. Then its mischief has the purest charm. And so it's especially hard for a mother to lose a child of that age. This one was still telling tales of her child fifty years later; he must have been lovable beyond the common run.

Just when she thought she must go mad with the pain, the next one knocked inside her belly for the first time. "Be still, you," she thought resentfully. Then it began to kick and flail. Now, all this thrashing around made too stark a contrast with the huge peace that streamed from the child in his coffin. It made the mother angry: "I don't like you, I don't want you"—and on and on in that way until she talked herself into hating the child that was coming. When it was time, she refused to think about bringing in some woman to help with the lying-in. She didn't want to hear about having the little white-bread eggs baked that new mothers ate in those parts; the father wanted still less to trim the chaise for a baptism, or even to hitch up the wagon in the grand style to fetch the midwife.

When it started, the mother crawled off to be alone. But then it came on full force and she was afraid. "You could bleed to death," she realized, and she thought of her husband and the half-dozen children she did have. So she sent for the neighbor woman, who helped.

The little thing turned out to be a female. The mother was glad of that. Its ugliness pleased her too. A lump with two holes in it was supposed to be the nose in this crumpled face. Forehead it had none, for right over the eyes sprouted an unsightly brown tuft of bristles. And since it had no neck either, the bristles ran down its back like a mane. Its toes and fingers were stubby; you had to look closely to be sure that they weren't crippled. Perhaps the mother wouldn't have grudged it to the creature if they had been crippled. No, this child had nothing in common with her lovely slain one.

Naturally the mother did her duty by the infant. She suckled it, and meanwhile it smacked greedily at her breasts. She groomed it, and when she did, she saw that the child observed its surroundings attentively. To her comings and goings it reacted surprisingly young, laughing or crying with special ardor, more ardor than the previous children had shown. So she began to like it a little.

The weird horse's mane gave way by degrees to a normal head of hair. Then the others could bear to mind the creature too.

The mother was looking forward again to her next child. She knew from the start that it would be a boy. Yes, he even looked like the other one, and got his name. And so they had him back again.

It was remarkable: After the bristly little animal, the mother gave birth to just as many children as she had had before; for she was one of those who simply had the children as they came. All were handsome, strapping children once again. And they were most welcome.

Worm

Hermine's first memory is of the wrinkled face of a nana, of a father's bad-tempered scowl and the angry faces of sisters and brothers who were struck and struck back. There was only one ray of light among them: the face of her mother. But this was always turning away again to someone else. Hermine might well have cried too much. It was said she was the most terrible whiner.

A somewhat later memory is of stomach-ache; stomach-ache before eating and the same again after eating; stomach-ache at night and stomach-ache in the morning. Mother with her comparisons said Hermine was growing too slowly and had black rings around her eyes. Therefore she gave her rainbow-colored worm-seed to eat by the spoonful. Although Hermine was already going behind the house—there, next to the high wooden privy, was a much littler one—now she had to go again in the potty, so that Mother could see if her "sowing" had sprouted. One day Hermine ran from it screaming. She had seen a worm, a monster of a worm. It had eyes, and a mouth as well, with teeth. She claimed it even had claws. Of course no one believed her about that, but even Mother said she had never seen such a thing in her life. Hermine's brother said she was wormy. After that, for a while, she shuddered at her own self.

Calf

Hermine got strange swellings on both sides of her forehead. "She's growing horns," said her father. For days on end, maybe even for weeks, the first thing she felt for every morning was her forehead, to see if they had punched through yet, her horns. Now Hermine could make comparisons. Right where you went from the house into the barn stood the calves who were still being nursed by the cows. Hermine, to be sure, was not particularly fond of the calves, who butted their mothers in the udders with disgusting roughness when they suckled. But now Hermine stroked them and compared; one calf she always felt first, for this one seemed to be about as far along as she was. One morning she had a bad scare: The little calf's horns had broken through—to this day Hermine can feel those tender spikes in her hands. In horror she reached for her own forehead, and got from the calf a hefty butt in the breast. Either the creature was sick of the perpetual groping or his head didn't itch him anymore. Hermine fell backwards onto the hard barn floor. The thickenings on her forehead soon went away, but now she often had headaches. From this time on, she managed to fall on her head again and again, especially when it was slippery outside. The headache was worst when she came into the warmth of the stove from the barnyard or when she did a somersault. Then it was like a knife through her head. For a long time afterwards she had to leave off jumping rope after the fifth jump, even though she could have gone on much longer.

Dog

The neighbor woman had a dog, handsome Barry. Everyone praised him for his sharp eye, his good nature and above all his love of children. The woman herself was childless. All the children who lived in the little village came by to show themselves how much Barry liked them. Hermine's sister even rode on him, for he was bigger than a calf. And so one time Hermine, too, dared to put out a timid hand to pet his great neck. Although the woman generally laughed at the fooleries that children carried on with the dog, she pulled Hermine away in sudden fear. From the deep bottom of the dog's soul there rose a growl, threatening, like distant thunder. He hadn't bitten her, but he snapped at her, and Hermine looked into the jaws of hell. Before her eyes she saw blue-black depths, and fire-red hanging things, and poison-yellow tufts, and pointy snow-white notches. Afterwards she cried out in her sleep at night. Father had to get up. And since she wasn't sick, he threw her ill-naturedly into bed with her mother.

Pig

Until she was about five, Hermine even had curls. The ringlets are pretty, they said. But they said it as if they were puzzled that she of all people should have them, as if they really didn't suit her. Meanwhile, because of the ringlets she had to suffer much, mostly when her nana combed them. Nana yanked. Every tangle, she said, came from a sin that Hermine had done. And when Hermine's big sister crocheted a red cap for her, she couldn't tell the real size of Hermine's head under the curls. The hat hung too loose. Hermine didn't like that. One day the children were making a snowman and it even fell off a few times. When the snowman was half done, Mother came and said: "If you can be as quiet as little mice, I'll let you see something lovely." For they had had pigs, as the saying goes: that is, they had had very good luck. The old mother sow had farrowed not ten, not twelve, but seventeen piglets. The children stood along the wall of the sty without making a sound. Hermine hung there more than stood, since she was turning out to be short. She had to do a sort of chin-up to pull herself onto the railing.

Their mother hadn't promised too much; they were very beautiful, all those curly little pigtails. Hermine liked it especially well that, in spite of having so many children, the pig still had a few teats free by her hind legs. The old sow lay there peacefully, saying "Oink" at regular intervals, and the little ones smacked their lips. Then, either to get a better position or because their little bellies were full, a few began to turn away from the mother's breast. The brother next to Hermine remembered the half-finished snowman, and he turned away too. As he did, he brushed the too-loose red cap with his elbow. Anyway, that's what Hermine said later. He said it wasn't so at all. Since Hermine, sadly, hadn't a free hand to hold it quickly in place, the cap fell right on the mother pig's snout. The old sow became a wild boar. She sprang up, ran around crazily in circles, uttered terrible sounds, trampled her children, seized the cap and threw it in the air, hurled it down and tore it to pieces. She confused it with her rosy pink children and bit a few of them to shreds too. The piglets and the children screamed. Their mother took a broom and saved what she could, pushing what was left into one corner. When the sow quieted down again, only nine little piglets were still alive.

Her father gave Hermine a sound thrashing. But what was much worse than that: her mother didn't like her anymore. Now if Hermine accidentally spilled her milk, Mother would say: "Just you wait, I'll throw you to the bad sow." For that was what they called the animal ever after. Once Hermine had a difference of opinion with the same brother. He pulled her hair, and she yelled. Then Mother grabbed her by the forearm and was about to make the worst come true. Hermine resigned herself to her fate; it was bound to happen some time. She went along, without resistance, towards the pigsty. While they were on the way, she imagined how the bad sow would carry on with her head: exactly as she had with the cap, she tossed it in the air, flung it down and bit it to pieces. Reproachfully, almost angrily, Hermine whispered to herself: "And my pretty ringlets, too!" Mother stopped short; then she laughed loud and long. That was the last time she threatened to throw Hermine to the bad pig.

Bear

One day a Gypsy wagon drove into the farmyard. A bear came along behind it, bound on a very short lead, with a basket over his muzzle. All the children who were there that day, and Mother too, arranged themselves on the big front stoop. It looked as if there'd be something to see. An old Gypsy climbed down from the seat farthest up front. He had an iron rod in his hand. An old Gypsy woman remained sitting there. She had a sleeping child on her lap, and acted as if all of this had nothing to do with her. The old man untied the bear, and suddenly there were two more Gypsies. Hermine hadn't seen when or how they had climbed down out of the wagon. These Gypsies were still young; the man had a violin, and the woman seemed very beautiful to Hermine. Now she began to make music: she swung around a ring of little bells. At the same time she swept the farmyard with her long skirt. When the young man began to play the violin, it sounded so ugly that Hermine was ashamed for him. The bear stood on all fours with his head hanging down; the old man poked him in the hindparts with his rod. When the bear sat back on that end of himself, Hermine started with fear at the size of the animal. It looked to her as if his head was much too small for his giant body. Most of all she didn't like his tiny little eyes. They seemed to be looking down in malice straight at her, and only at her.

By now the music was loud and fast. The bear-tamer poked him again, and this time the bear started to dance: he took steps up and back, turned himself this way and that and swung his paw with the beat. This was all very fine and everyone was pleased.

The old Gypsy took a shorter hold of the bear. But as if this were part of the dance the animal took too long a step and reached out too far with his paw. He swung at Hermine. The huge claws swept down just under her eyes, but luckily she only got a rip in her apron. The music stopped on a beat. The bear howled. Mother pushed the children hastily into the house and bolted the door. Otherwise she did that only at night. And then through the front window they saw and heard the most amazing uproar. The bear was down on all fours again, on his short lead. The old Gypsy beat him with the iron rod, the young man yanked at the horse. Just as she had done earlier with the ring of little bells, the beautiful Gypsy now swung around the screaming child. The old woman did the worst thing of all. She shrieked in a foreign tongue. And so, only a little after she had heard her first violin, Hermine heard for the first time a foreign language. She didn't like either one of them. At last, the old woman came to the window and begged in queer German, "Moo-ther, Moo-ther." Mother gave her half a loaf of bread, which, it seems, was too little. Grumbling their discontent, they went on their way. They were the last bear tamers that anyone ever saw in those parts.

Father cursed Hermine: "That one would have to stand out in front of everybody." But Hermine had a brother who tried to come to her aid. He said: "Hermine wasn't standing out front, and not up top or down at the bottom either. She was right in the middle." But Father didn't want to hear it.

Cow

Through all the years of her childhood, Hermine had one great worry. The feeding alley in the barn, which lay in between the row of cows and the row of horses and younger cattle, was the nightly meeting place of the children. But in order to get to it you had to force a narrow passage on one side or the other. Neither the front cow nor the front horse was willing to let Hermine through; they wouldn't give and that was that. She might manage it by pressing in close behind her sisters and brothers, or better yet between them. Or by stealth. Then she waited until the cow was eating so greedily she no longer paid Hermine any mind, or until she fought over a wisp of fodder with her neighbor. Should the cow spot her afterwards in the feeding alley, she shook her head in rage and took better care next time to back Hermine off with her great muzzle or even with her horns.

    The horse gave her even more trouble. He had ways all his own of stopping Hermine: He could neigh at her furiously, prick up his ears and stamp his hooves, blow out so that his nostrils quivered and the wet oats flew down the back of Hermine's neck; he could show her his long yellow teeth. Once he caught her by the hair on her crown and yanked her high in the air. When she screamed piteously, Father made fun of her and the horse laughed his hideous laugh. On that side she gave up trying altogether.

Once again a brother, a different one, looked out for Hermine, seeing how she tried in vain to get around the obstacle of the cow. He was younger than she but a good deal cleverer. "You're going about it wrong," he said. "The cow notices something about you. You have to act as though she isn't there at all." Then he said something even wise: "You don't have to show any respect for cattle. They have no reason and no immortal soul." And so Hermine tried arrogance. Slowly, proudly, holding her head high, she tried to make her way, but the cow completely blocked the passageway with her thick head. Not until the clever brother struck her across the wet muzzle with a stick would she let Hermine pass.

Crow

Early one summer, Mother had three fine flocks of chicks. She said one evening: "One brood is missing two little chicks, and another is short three." From then on, she had a similar complaint every night. The little children were instructed to look out for the evildoer, for the older ones were hard at work in the field. And so they stood watch in groups of three or four about the chickenyard. Suddenly the rooster stretched out his neck and began to cackle with wild excitement. The chickens scattered and flew squawking under the protection of the roofs. In horror the three mother hens clucked to gather their children under their wings. The chicks came running as well as they could, but they were still small and stupid. A giant crow hopped down from the pear tree and pecked one to death. She did this before the eyes of the children, then flapped off serenely with her prey to the nearby edge of the woods. She probably had hungry children of her own in the nest.

Not that the watchmen had looked on speechlessly all this while. They clapped and screamed and came running, but the crow paid them no mind. The children ran crying to the field. "It's a big disgusting crow, bold as anything," they shouted. Father was angry. "What's the use of having all these brats? They can't even get the better of a bird." Since Hermine was crying the loudest, she got the slap in the head.

Meanwhile the crow snatched two more chicks. She must be a clever one, with some years on her too, Mother said. When the grownups were about the place, she didn't come. She often snatched a chick while they were at dinner. One brood hen had only two children left; it was a pitiful sight. Mother set a new hen to roost over some eggs, although she knew that such late chicks would never make good layers.

Every Sunday Father lay in ambush with his rifle for the crow, but in vain. There was no end to the slaughter of the chicks; by now the old crow had it all figured out. Word of their misfortune got around.

The neighbors had a hired man. In February, not long after Candlemas when they had taken him on, they were already saying to him: "At Martinmas you can be on your way again." They were displeased with him because he was a puny, skinny little man who neither could nor would do the heavy work of the farm. Hermine wondered at him, since he was cheerful all the same. At night he played his harmonica, on Sundays he took the children for rides on his bicycle. His name was Jakob, and he was still gladly playing the fool with the children. He bought an airgun out of his wages and shot at sparrows with it. His aim was good, and of sparrows they had more than enough. One afternoon Jakob, doing nothing himself, took up with the hapless children. He laid his airgun on the ground and played at high jump with them. Then came the clucking and squawking. The crow sat in the pear tree. She hopped down fast from branch to branch, as if the tree were a flight of stairs. Jakob yelled and clapped his hands with the children. But when the crow was on the lowest branch, quick as lightning he snatched up his airgun and shot her. Then he climbed up into the pear tree with the dead crow and hung her, with a rope for binding wheat sheaves, from the highest branch.

This dead crow was a horror for Hermine. She couldn't stop looking up at it. Soon the hank of black feathers was nothing like a crow anymore. Sometimes it looked like a devil, sometimes again like a hideous human face or a cat. At night Hermine had bad dreams of the crow. In November, about Martinmas, a strong fall wind finally tore the light corpse loose and blew it away. By then Jakob was gone as well.

Pigeons

Hermine's special brother had his every wish fulfilled. Luckily he didn't have many wishes. But he did want pigeons. As if they didn't have enough creatures about the place! On Sunday Father hammered together a dovecote under the roof. He brought home a splendid pair of pigeons from the market. They were purebred, he said. Anybody could see this, for they glinted golden-brown and had white neckbands. The brother often climbed the steep little ladder in the uppermost loft to the dovecote and attended to the brooding and the laying. He was disappointed, though, in the young ones: they were so ugly that he said it made him sick to look at them.

One Saturday evening, Hermine sat alone on the rear stoop of the house. That she was alone was already astonishing. That almost never happened. She sat with her head tilted to one side, as she almost always did, and watched the pigeons. The chickens were already in the barn, but the pigeons were still dancing around the hens' water. They cooed, bowed to each other, and rode on top of one another. Despite her youth Hermine sensed that they already had their next ugly brood in mind.

Father was sweeping the street. It pleased him to do that every Saturday evening, for he was a lover of order. That's left over from his years as a soldier, said Mother. At night, if the children hadn't set their shoes exactly in a row according to size underneath the bench by the stove, he bellowed frightfully: "What a pigsty!" Also on Saturday afternoons all their Sunday shoes had to be set out in a precise row for cleaning, with his at the top of the row, and the daughter who polished his shoes till they gleamed was dear to his heart. Hermine sat all this while looking on at the strange doings of the pigeons.

Then her blood froze. Still a fair distance off, the cat came creeping. She moved no more than an inch at a time, her murderous glance fixed hard on the pigeons. The birds noticed nothing, and afterwards Hermine could never understand why she hadn't simply chased them out of the danger zone. Instead, entirely under the spell of what was happening, she crept up to Father and whispered: "The cat." At once he leaned the broom against the wall and fetched his rifle from the storeroom. It would have pleased him to shoot his gun often, if only he had had an excuse. He would been glad to shoot the crow, for one. That too was left over from his years as a soldier. But now he had to take aim fast. The cat was quite close to the unsuspecting pigeons. There was a bang, and all of them were dead: the cat and the pigeons too. It was a shotgun.

Everybody came running. The crying and screaming were terrific. Mother cried: "You just can't stand it when anything gives me pleasure." For she had liked that cat; it was a good mouser. Father didn't know what excuse to make for himself, other than that Hermine had told him to shoot. The brother with the pigeons cried miserably; Father gave him the same comfort. Everyone was angry with Hermine. In bed she sobbed; for the first time she wished that she was dead too—she wished it until she fell asleep.

But the next day was Sunday. The parents spoke to each

other again in normal voices. Before they sat down to eat, Hermine's brother had forgiven her, for when he went to throw the ugly, frozen, starving young ones out of the nest, four beautiful pigeons, all with neckbands, were cowering there before his wide-open eyes. They flew out of the dovecote and pecked at stray grains along with the chickens, just as the old ones had. Mother had her Sunday gossip with the neighbor woman, and brought home a new cat. Only Father was still angry at Hermine. And yet he had every reason to forgive her, for soon he had an excuse to shoot as much as he liked. As highborn and purebred as the four pigeons were, they didn't hold with inbreeding. They brought home marriage partners of the commonest sort. Their young ones had grayish spots or were plain gray-blue. Of the characteristic neckband of the purebred bird, only bits and pieces could be seen. Behind their sheer numbers, too, there was a disgusting haste, and Hermine's brother had no objection if Father shot at them at will.

Rooster

Hermine's big sister was pretty. Nearly all the boys in the neighborhood were under her spell. Every Saturday night she wanted to be the one to catch the rooster, for from July until late in the fall they would slaughter a cock every Sunday. Cunningly she scattered grain to the rooster flock and then seized the handsomest. The poor fellow fluttered and shrieked. But then she took chalk and made a circle on the front stoop. She laid the excited animal in the middle of it. There it lay, as still as death, without even being held, and stared cross-eyed at the chalk line. That's what a witch she was. Then a brother had to hang onto the legs. She flattened the cock's neck on the chopping block and struck the handsome head off with her ax. She always managed to do this with one blow. The head lay on the dung heap; she held the rooster upside-down above it to let the blood run out. Then she threw him in an old tub. Inside of it he jumped around in a headless frenzy. She watched and laughed at him, down to his last twitch. That's what a hangman's wife she was!

At Sunday dinner, she wanted a big piece of him, to be exact the piece with the fat pope's-nose. That was her style. Their father wanted the neck. Two brothers wanted drumsticks; two others wanted wings. Sisters who were doing some work about the place got white meat. Their mother, Hermine, and sundry other useless ones got stuffing. But their mother knew how to make stuffing very well indeed. What wouldn't fit inside the cock she simply roasted next to it.

Cleaning the rooster fascinated Hermine. For that she actually stood in front of the others to watch. First of all, the changes moved her. A thing that had been lustrous and full of colors turned black and dreary in the hot water. Once plucked, it looked small and naked. If the poor creature went over the open fire so they could strip away the last bits of down, Hermine always imagined her own likely cleansing in the flames of purgatory, or even the torments of hell. And later it was thrilling because exactly the same things came out of every rooster once Mother cut it open and reached inside. She had to be very careful not to rupture the gall sac, for if that should happen, she said, the meat is no good to eat anymore. Luckily it never occurred.

This gall sac, a little greenish-black thing, the rosy red lungs and the blue intestines all went to the neighbor's dog. He had already eaten the head and now was waiting at the bottom of the stairs. Hermine's parents didn't have a dog themselves, since Mother was squeamish. She couldn't bear to watch, she said, when children ate bread-and-butter and petted a dog at the same time. Now she cut open the rooster's gizzard and rinsed out a little heap of grains. Hermine always felt sorry for it then, since the creature had eaten all that for nothing. The small heart she regarded with awe. The liver she wanted to reach out quickly and touch: it gleamed wetly, and yet it was dry. It was great fun; it was also what made the stuffing taste so good. Last of all, with force, their mother pulled the dead rooster's crop out of the wrinkled neck. The crop, too, Hermine wanted to touch, to feel the little pebbles and the grains that he'd eaten up just before.

Mother had a crop too—a goitre. Once Hermine heard them say that it came from the pains of childbirth, from the part when the child was pressing. From ferocious childbirth, from the pains before and the pains after, her mother had varicose veins. You rarely saw them, because Mother wore thick black stockings summer and winter. The goitre, too, she hid cleverly under the high, stiff collars of her dresses. But now, for the hot work of cleaning the rooster, her top button was open. Hermine's fingers itched to glide over it, to see if she could feel there the bit of bread and hard black sausage that Mother had been nibbling on earlier. But touching wasn't the custom with them. She could barely recall pressing her cheek, once, shyly, against her mother's. There was nothing like that between sisters and brothers. Only the baby you might pet a little, when no one was looking. With their father, every touch was unthinkable. Oh, certainly he might pick up a two-year-old in his arms, or lead a three-year-old by the hand. But after that you only came in contact with Father's hand when you were getting a beating. Granted that wasn't often, with Hermine somewhat oftener than with the others, but the hand was hard as wood. Once Hermine couldn't help herself: she softly drew her forefinger across Mother's goitre and told her father why. Mother liked to laugh at Hermine and didn't mind being laughed at herself. She told that story everywhere. Only Father didn't laugh.

Turkey

Father almost went too far with Hermine: he gave her away. Not exactly for Christmas, but shortly after it, to an uncle and an aunt on a farm where there were no children. Not that she was ever supposed to get this farm. Rather, she had to go there in place of the brother who had been chosen for that, because the brother didn't want to move to his uncle's just yet. At first Hermine liked it. She was allowed to have Christmas cookies, all she could eat. On New Year's Day it began to snow, and then came magnificent winter weather. After the midday dinner Hermine said, "Now they're sledding." So her uncle dropped everything, drove into the city and bought her a sled. It wasn't his fault that he had no hill. Just along the street there was a bit of a slope. She tried various places on various days. It wouldn't slide right. Hermine comforted herself: Back home it wasn't so wonderful either. There they had to sit four or five to a sled. So that the ones in back could steer, she had to sit all the way up front, because she was the smallest. When she got scared during the wild ride downhill and tried to slow them down, the snow went up under her skirt. Woolen slip and shirt would be wet up to her chin. And then again in the evening, when uncle and aunt were at work in kitchen and barn, Hermine comforted herself: at home now they were throwing each other off the bench in front of the stove and fighting for a warm seat. Here she had a whole stove to herself. She sat on the bench and tried out different places again and again. Meanwhile she wasn't even wet or cold.

When the snow melted, she thought how back home now they were running around looking for snowdrops. Far more of them grew here than there, and she picked a bunch again and again. But soon the aunt was scolding: She had run out of vases for flowers. Then the aunt bought her a ball. But what can a girl of some five years old do all alone with a ball? In the end she let it roll into the puddle by the dung heap and there it stayed.

When the blackbirds sang in the evening, Hermine got sad. "Now they're allowed to go out and play till dark," she thought.

Her uncle brought her home a scooter from the city. But it wasn't uncle's fault that at his place everything was soft and the narrow wooden wheels sank in. Back home the farmyard was plenty hard. "Don't be such a whiner, there are paving stones all along the dung heap, you can ride there," her aunt scolded. And Hermine rode, up and down and up and down again. The spring air can make you sick, so the aunt said. She bought her a little red jacket. Nobody at home would ever have thought of such a thing, neither of the unhealthy spring air, nor of the new jacket. Hermine started across the farmyard. The aunt had begun her garden, and Hermine wanted to watch. Whatever her mother did, the aunt did it differently, and did it all wrong. The turkeys were out in the farmyard. Hermine had not taken to these animals. They didn't have any back home, and she didn't like their naked warty heads and necks. Because it was spring the turkey was in a great uproar. He jerked and lurched, spread out his feathers and his tail, blushed fiery red in his wattles. Hermine cut a wide circle around him. She thought she had gotten by. He flew at her from behind and pecked at her head. She fell down in terror. The turkey was just as frightened and ran away. Hermine screamed bloody murder. You couldn't blame the aunt for finally saying in exasperation: "That turkey never ate anybody yet." But now Hermine wouldn't stop crying and sobbing out "Home, home." The whole grief over the lost winter and the lost half a spring burst out of her.

Then you couldn't think any worse of the aunt that she rolled the wheelbarrow in front of the front stoop, turned the sled over on top of it and stuffed Hermine's things between the runners. The pretty little jacket was one of them. Hermine tried to hold onto it so she could wear it home; her aunt said: "No need for you to look all that grand." On top of the pile she laid the scooter. Last of all she fetched the ball out of the dung water puddle with a rake.

So Hermine never got any part of this inheritance. If she had stayed there, everything could have come out differently, for that brother died young. Therefore one can say without saying too much that the turkey drove her off from her inheritance. Mother combed the lice out of her ringlets, and Father never talked to her at all anymore, but only about her. He said: "That one's worth nothing to God and the whole world."

Ducks

That spring her mother handed over to her the care of the ducks. The year before you started school, you were big enough to bear the responsibility. The word pleased Hermine uncommonly. She made up her mind to be worthy of the responsibility. Therefore she started to look after the ducks the moment they were hatched. That wouldn't have been strictly necessary, for at first the brood-hen was there. Once she had the duck eggs from a neighbor woman, Mother would slip them under the first hen that began to sit. The neighbor was so rich she could have ducks year round. But Mother needed feathers mostly in late autumn for all the feather-beds, and more pressingly needed the cash that city people would lay out for roast duck.

Not only the brood hen but Mother, too, was taking care of the ducklings: she soaked white bread for them and put bran mash and sometimes even chopped eggs in their trough. Now Hermine could prove herself worthy of her responsibility. For all day long the brood-hen would be hard at it to fight off her sister chickens from the duck trough. Hermine could tell by looking at the hens even from a distance what they were up to, and helped the foster mother. Sometimes Hermine got disgusted with her: when all the ducklings had their heads under their wings, the brood-hen herself would gulp down a few tasty morsels.

Hermine was entirely on the side of the ducklings, especially since the little row of them was so wonderfully pretty to look at. Suddenly there was a great clamor in the chickenyard. Hermine ran quick, to restore justice and order. The brood-hen was making a dreadful fuss, for her ill-bred children were not only drinking the water for the chickens but swimming in it. This time Hermine couldn't help her, since you mustn't come too close to a hen who's in such a state.

Now that they were being spoiled from every side, the ducklings grew fast. Their foster mother would have liked to show off her flourishing brood all around, as every mother hen does with her chicks. But once again there wasn't much Hermine could do to assist her; for ducks are not fond of exercise and would just as soon plump down lazily beside the feeding trough with their crops stuffed full. This time Hermine was more on the side of the hen again, and felt sorry for her when she tried to entice them with kernels of grain, worms, and even with glistening pebbles, all in vain.

Then came that rainy May morning. The brood-hen wanted to stay under the overhanging roof of the barn, but the flock of ducklings stretched their beaks forth and waddled, one after the other as if pulled on strings, straight down the path towards the pond. Hermine was responsible and went with them at a certain distance. The hen was in a bad way. That far from the barnyard no chicken ever goes. She ran in front of them and then again in back of them, cackled and clucked and hissed at Hermine and her children by turns. The ducklings paid no attention. By the straightest route they arrived at the pond and splashed in. Now the hen was at her wit's end: she raced wildly up and down the shore. Hermine feared for her reason. She picked up a long stick to drive the ducklings out of the water. The hen understood this all wrong: she flew in Hermine's face and gave her a nasty scratch on the upper lip. Mother put schnapps on it, so that it hurt even more, and observed besides: "There's no need to come in that close, you know."

Then the hen lost her maternal instinct overnight. Hermine could understand it: you don't willingly go through a thing like that twice. She saw that the brood-hen even gobbled up everything in the duck trough with the other chickens. Now Hermine knew that her time had come. Every day she spent long hours at the pond with her ducks. Or she ran down there again and again, so that fox and hawk would see that the ducklings were under guard. In the evening she drove them all home to the barn. At first the number of them gave her some trouble. Since the brood-hen had been extra large, Mother had pushed under her, back before Easter, not seven but nine new duck eggs. But soon Hermine had it worked out: five were swimming here and four there, or six paddled and three slept, or seven ruffled their feathers on shore, one was swimming in the middle, and Hermine was still looking and already she suspected the fox of the worst—there came the ninth out from under a big leaf. The ducks throve under Hermine's protection. She saw: they were six ducks and three drakes. Now there were even more counting games. Everything went well, it was lovely, and Hermine's sisters and brothers came down for the sheer fun of it.

By now it was high summer, and when she came in the evening to fetch them, the six ducks stood ready to march; two drakes had not had enough of swimming yet. But where was the third? She looked up and down. She called, *"Guss, guss!"* Then, in a place where there was really no ground to stand on, she saw a pile of feathers. So the fox had snatched one after all. Hermine wept. She sank in up to her knees to save what little she could, and gathered a handful of iridescent feathers. By then the ducklings were gone. When Hermine got home, they were satisfying the last of their hunger at the duck trough. They didn't take the death of their brother too much to heart. Then Hermine noticed her own hunger and took fright. Because of the feathers, she was late, and now all the brown butter from the browned porridge would surely be gone. When she arrived at the table, the case was even more serious. The pot was empty and they were licking the spoons. Maybe Hermine looked comical with her smeared and tear-stained face, her muddy legs and a tuft of feathers in her hand. Or else what she said was odd and made a funny match with the licking of spoons. "The fox ate him after all," was all she said. Everyone laughed, loud and long. When their father had laughed enough, he said: "Let's be glad he didn't eat her." And Mother: "Those ducks have been big enough a long time already. They can find their own way home."

So Hermine was relieved of her responsibility, with laughter and scorn, and hungry into the bargain. Father had his place at table directly in front of the bread drawer. Hermine didn't dare ask him to move out of the way. So she went outside, threw the bunch of feathers on the dung heap, washed her face and legs at the well trough and went to the early apples. Summer was far enough gone so that they had begun to fall. But the fallen, early-ripened apples had already found customers. Hermine reached and stretched and jumped for an unripe one. That night it gave her a terrible stomach-ache. She knew that green apples could kill you. In her fear she woke the sister who was sleeping in the same room. The sister only rolled over on her other side: "Just go to Father," she said. For if something hurt at night, they went to their father. Mother wanted her rest, and Father couldn't sleep anyway, because of his own stomach-ache. But Hermine was still ashamed in front of her father. She put up with the cramps until she fell asleep.

Geese

The teacher hadn't heard about Hermine. He treated her like anybody else. She liked that. She didn't make all that much work for him, since, thanks to the ducks, she knew her numbers very well as far as ten. And when it came to tens, hundreds, and even thousands—as she heard when the big boys and girls did their lessons, for all seven school years sat in the same room—she was hugely disappointed that it just went on and on in the same track. She had expected more out of school. Words and letters came to her as no great marvel either, since she had older sisters and brothers. So she was allowed to stay after school to help with the dumb ones, who had no choice but to stay after.

Now this made a problem for Hermine. The dumb ones didn't live in the direction where the big farms were but rather in the village, where the tavern was and the store and the factory where their fathers went to work. Thus Hermine had to walk the whole way home alone. Along the way a farmer's wife had a flock of geese. These knew all about Hermine and had it in for her, and she feared them like the devil incarnate. They stretched out their long necks, hissed, tugged at her apron, and nipped her in the calves. Her sisters and brothers took her by in the middle of them. But if she was alone she often had to wait a while, pretending she was looking for flowers or pebbles, until the geese were in the water. If this took too long she just ran by like a crazy person. The farmhands stood at the barn door and laughed at her.

Luckily, in Hermine's second year of school, the farmer's wife switched from geese to ducks.

Cats

The new cat wasn't what the old one had been, the one who had been shot. She didn't even know she had to keep her kittens hidden away until they were handsome and could lap milk by themselves. Only then the old mother cat used to pick them up by the back of the neck and carry them one at a time to the sun-warmed front stoop. But first she showed the kittens off proudly, one after the other, to Mother. And just as quick, Mother told Father to kill them, before the children had a chance to play with them, for she wished to spare the children needless heartache. Afterwards the old cat searched about for a time in house and barn, then went back to catching mice.

The new cat, for her part, fixed up a bed for her lying-in in the old cupboard that stood in the upstairs hall. This was so old that the doors no longer locked. The cat pushed the door open with an adroit paw, and if anyone looked inside, she hissed angrily. One day she didn't come back to the house, not in the morning, not in the afternoon, not in the evening. The worst must have happened to her. A cat doesn't leave five hungry children to their fate for no reason. Hermine and her sister, whose room was right next to the cat's cupboard, tried to sleep but couldn't. The pitiful mewing of the kittens swelled through the silent house. Hermine couldn't stand it any longer; she went and got the little things. *Hu,* they were ugly. Big naked heads with blind frog-eyes in them, and bright pink claws and rat tails, they wound themselves in a hungry clump on Hermine's bed cover. She ran down fast to the kitchen and got the cat's dish. There was still milk in it for the one who hadn't come back. Hermine dipped the dreadful little heads in the milk. "But they can't drink any cold milk," said her sister, and rolled over as usual to her other side. That seemed logical to Hermine: even to the old cat they had used to give only warmed-up milk, or milk still warm from the cow. So Hermine hastened into the kitchen and made a small fire of kindling in the stove. She climbed on a kitchen chair and lifted the big brass pan down from the shelf. The cat's milk looked stingy in it. She added some from the milk jug. Just as the milk began to steam, the clock in the room struck twelve. Fear of her dead ancestors overtook Hermine. Trembling, she poured the milk into the saucer. The kittens turned away from the warm milk too. Hermine wetted their heads with it so they would at least lick each other off. Back in the cupboard they mewed even louder than before. Now Hermine's sister, who had a healthy relation to animals, got sick of this nonsense. From the third step down she flung them, one kitten after the other, with all her strength, against the hard stone floor. Then there was peace, and they could sleep.

Mother, who slept in a small room nearby, woke up. For an awful stink had come leaking around the edges of the door and through the keyhole: the little fire of kindling wood had ignited a charred log in the stove. The beautiful brass pan was probably ruined. "I ought to beat you over the head with all five of them," Mother screamed at Hermine in the morning, and she picked up one of the ugly dead kittens. The horror in Hermine's face must have made Mother think better of this plan. The pan soaked in the rainwater barrel for a long time. As soon as

Hermine got out of school, she scratched away at it. But Mother rubbed the metal again and again with sand and a handful of straw. Finally she tried salt and essence of vinegar and at last the pan came clean.

Frog

Since there was a pond close to the farmhouse, the children could sometimes do something to please the teacher. The boys caught salamanders and gold-edged diving beetles, both highly prized for educational demonstrations. Hermine's quick sister once even caught a dragonfly. It's true that it gave up all its shining glamor to the one who was showing it off, for it sat there in a shoebox punched with holes like some gray-black fossil from the dawn of time. The highest praise, though, was reserved for those who brought tadpoles, ones with tails, or better yet front legs. Then the teacher had a lot to talk about. About development, about breathing through gills and lungs: he went on and on about all that just as if he had invented this wonder of nature himself.

Hermine was not the quickest, but one time she had great luck. She caught a tadpole with tail, back legs and front legs. She could hardly sleep, she was so eager to hand this scientific evidence and conversation piece over to the teacher. Right after morning prayer she gave it to him in a glass of water. But the teacher had arithmetic in mind. And so he put it aside on the sunlit window sill without a word. Just before recess he remembered about the glass. But it was empty. Even the teacher was embarrassed; he poked around for quite a while with a slate pencil, looking for a tail. But the tail had probably dissolved in the water, and the tiny frog must have developed in those two hours and become extinct again, somewhere in the row of rough shoes. "Water show-off, glass show-off," her classmates made fun of her. She might have known.

Deer

Close by the schoolhouse was a tumbledown shack. Here lived Kitz, who, despite the name, was more of a strange bird than a kid or a fawn. Nobody knew exactly what he lived on. He had a big garden. Sometimes he did odd jobs. In the spring and fall he caught mice in the farmers' fields and meadows. He showed the same mice to more than one farmer; that way he got on not too badly and was free to roam about in the woods. To the teacher this neighbor was an eyesore. Nevertheless he admonished his pupils not to call him "Hey Kitz" but rather "Herr Kitz." Kitz had nothing against the schoolchildren. He even let them pet his nanny goat. Nice little girls like Hermine's sister he called "dear heart." One day Kitz really did have a *kitz*—a fawn. It became the delight of the schoolchildren. When they called, it came running to them, and let itself be petted and fed. After summer vacation, Hansi—that's what they called him—was still there. The children were amazed what a big deer he had become in the meantime. All the same he came when they called, and they saw that the white spots on his back had almost disappeared. Two pointy horns stuck out of his head. Even so he let them pet him.

Just then Hermine noticed the peculiar, stiff way he lowered his head and twisted it at the same time. When he set his front legs in her direction, she tried to run away. And so she got a horn in her backside. It hurt very much. Everyone said she was lucky it was her behind, not her belly. As for her belly, she had to sleep on it, and in school she had to stand up. To the teacher this was a great nuisance. He had the local police tell Kitz either to get rid of the deer or to pen it up. Kitz did neither. But the children didn't call to Hansi anymore; he stood by the side of the little house, his feelings hurt. At last the teacher reported Kitz to the higher authorities. The ranger shot the young buck. Kitz didn't even get the meat. The children wailed about the deer for a long time. On top of that, Kitz was ordered to pay damages for pain and suffering. But Hermine's father renounced the claim, for her injury was long since healed; by now she could sit and sleep again however she wanted. Only the threatening fist that Kitz made at her sometimes took the joy out of life. That fall, Kitz caught no mice for them. But by springtime, he had forgotten the fist and was back at their mice as before.

Tomcat

Every second year came a school inspection. The girls put on new aprons, or at least freshly laundered ones. Besides the inspector of schools, Hermine's father was there, and so was a farmer from the next town who had almost as many children in the school. As the local school board, they leaned against the wall in back. The teacher gave a lesson on cats. The students interrupted noisily. On cats they were all experts. Hermine felt sorry for the floundering teacher, never mind if he really knew anything or not. She raised her finger and began to explain how cats' eyes worked, why they can see at night. Hermine's eagerness caught the attention of the inspector of schools. He asked her kindly: "And what do you call your kitty at home?" "Boole," she said—Tom Fool—not a very nice word, though it was the exact truth. For some years now they'd had no luck with female cats and had finally asked the neighbor for a tom—a big dumb Boole. But Hermine had said the all too fitting name a bit too promptly and loudly into the face of the inspector of schools. At home Father carried on dreadfully on account of the disgrace. Hermine raised the question whether the inspector of schools had even known she belonged to their family. That was the way she comforted them.

Pig

The pig in this case is the slaughtered pig. It's true there were only two of those in a year, one as winter was coming in, the other as winter was going out. Most of the family looked forward to it, but for Hermine these were days of affliction. It started already the night before, for the pig whose turn it was got nothing to eat. Hermine felt the deepest pity for that. Sometimes she managed to smuggle a sugar beet to the squealing animal without anyone seeing. And then in early morning came the horrible death cry. Hermine hid under the covers or held her hands over her ears. Later she didn't have to hear the death cry anymore, because the butcher bought a slaughtering gun. But something terrible happened with that too. True, not at their place, but at another farm where they slaughtered at night because the man of the house, who worked in a factory, wanted to be there. The butcher's apprentice shot himself instead of the pig. The policeman said that they had to leave him lying exactly where he was, meaning in the ramshackle laundry kitchen. They covered him with an old horse blanket. The rats ate away the nose, ears and fingertips of the poor young man. Hermine hadn't seen it. But it must have been a dreadful sight, for they told stories about it for a long time. After that she was terribly afraid, every time, that one of them, besides the pig, might not get out of there alive. Then she saw, from far away, the snow turn blood red.

Some of her siblings couldn't stand close enough when all that boiling and scraping and chopping was going on. Already at nine in the morning the first heap of bloody stuff arrived in the kitchen. Hermine went into the next room, but soon they came in behind her to eat the roasted liver. Hermine wouldn't have minded eating some of that, but the butchers had on bloody aprons, and what was worse, their hairy forearms too were covered with blood. So, taking an apple, she went to her aunt's. But soon the aunt had had enough of her and sent her home again. If the sow had been good and fat and so Mother was in high spirits, she made a pancake for Hermine for midday dinner and a fried egg for her supper. Otherwise Hermine ate a piece of bread, which didn't taste right to her since on these days it smelled of sauerkraut. The others ate *metzelsuppe* from all the chopped and boiled bits, although it was never really anything like a soup. The cousin was there, and they all laughed when Hermine's stomach turned over as soon as they started to press the clotted blood out of the gut casings.

The second day went by more quietly. The pig hung in two halves that reached from the ceiling to the floor, no matter how short and round it had been when living. In the evening the butcher came again, only now he was called the meat-cutter. As a matter of fact he had a lot of names. If Mother had a litter of piglets and the four-week-old baby boars had to be castrated, she called after one of the girls: "After school, make a date with the piglet-cutter." If there was a sick cow at the neighboring farm and they happened to see this man's car out front—for he had the first car in all the district—then someone said: "Now they've fetched the cow doctor." If he wasn't in church on Sunday, at the midday dinner there was speculation: "Weisshaupt must have gone to church in the city." As the meat-cutter he divided the pig into rectangular pieces. Hermine looked on, for now nothing bled anymore. Mother soaked these pieces in brine right away. Although it was cold when they arranged for the butcher, there was a thaw by the time he was the meat-cutter. In a clean new calves' pail he threw the feet, hocks, ears, snout and the bristly tail of the sow. One time Hermine suggested to Mother that they just throw that stuff away. Then the meat-cutter laughed at her so hard that ever after she was ashamed in front of him and didn't watch anymore. And so she was always glad, a little later, when all those jellied parts, bristles and all, had been eaten up. Then at least they had their own plates back again. Mother laid out for the meat-cutter every single big dish that she had. She added sausages and bones to the pieces of meat, and the children carried these slaughter-gifts to neighbors and kin. Hermine was happy at everything that went out of the house. Granted it all came back again when the neighbors slaughtered—at Epiphany, Candlemas or Shrovetide—sometimes, as people said of one neighbor woman, weighed to the last gram. But by then it didn't matter to Hermine, as long as the bacon didn't pile up anymore in such huge amounts.

But just now a willow basket full of bacon stood in the kitchen, and it was on account of the bacon that Hermine suffered her greatest affliction. For when the bacon was rendered, a disgusting odor penetrated the whole house. The table, her slateboard for school, even the bed seemed greasy. It made her ill, so that she couldn't eat. And when the lard pots were finally sealed up in the cellar, the misery was still not over. For there stood the rack with the pale, greasy, curing meat. The cat prowled around it. Nothing in the world would make Hermine go down in the cellar alone at such times. She couldn't go up in the loft under the roof either, if the meat was hanging in the chimney and the flue had to be opened or shut according to mother's orders. Only when the stripes of lean began to glisten blackish red did Hermine stop being afraid of it. Then she would even have eaten some. But since everyone knew that she couldn't stand anything from a pig, she got none. Once when they were taking around the Easter eggs, her aunt nagged her so long that she finally ate a little lard biscuit. It made her deathly ill. Before they went visiting, Mother gave her children special rules of behavior. Thus she said to one of them: "Just make sure you don't contradict a single little word I say." For this child was given to speaking the truth and nothing but the truth. To Hermine, Mother said: "And don't eat so much!" That bothered Hermine terribly. If she would at least have said "too much." That would have acknowledged that she had limits set by her own stomach. But this made her sound as gluttonous as a pig, and she made up her mind, whenever they were going to visit their relatives, not to eat anything at all. But she never quite managed to do it.

In school they had to write a composition: "Hurray, We're Slaughtering!" The others were already writing; Hermine wept. The teacher spoke to her kindly. Could it be she knew nothing of the subject? Oh she knew something about it, but only bad things. "Then just leave out the 'Hurray,'" the teacher said, but then he must have taken pity, knowing that it isn't easy for a fifth grader to write about ugly stuff for two hours straight. Hermine got a special subject: "Hurray, We're Making Cider!" She was grateful to the teacher. But as she got ready to write, there too only bad things came to mind. The cider mill was next to the room where they did the slaughtering; it was everywhere wet and cold. There she always wanted the seat in front of the oven where the bread was baked. Because Father sprayed the trees with Karbolineum only once, in very early spring, and for cider they used the windfalls, Hermine knew for sure that every apple had a fat worm in it. She didn't care for all that shredding and pressing of worms. She couldn't bring herself to drink even a swallow of sweet cider. Only once it was fermented did the worm juice seem to her fit to drink. But now she had to hurry and repay the teacher some way for his special treatment of her. She began to lie: the sacks of apples spilled over, her sister slipped on the rolling apples, fell head over heels in the mash. She herself sat on the wooden beam of the press and rode merrily back and forth. All the while she drank sweet cider by the liter. She came very near to describing a drunken orgy. Still, she invented only what was plausible. The teacher was very pleased with her. He even praised her in front of the others, and she turned fiery red.

Bull

They had a giant bull standing in their barn. When he was half grown he had already made himself the talk of the place. Once their father had had to fight a long time for air, for the bull had him pinned up against the barn wall. After that, they couldn't let the fellow loose anymore for breeding. And because of that, he got madder and madder. He had to be bound three ways. The usual chain around his neck was extra thick. On top of that he had one around the back of his muzzle, and from it ran two chains to rings in the neighboring stalls. So the big bull had little freedom of movement. If he lay down, he could only put his thick head down straight in front of him. All night, from deep inside him, he rumbled and roared. As far away as their bed chambers they heard him and were afraid. "Sell that big bull at last, before something else happens," their mother often said to their father. But Father saw that the bull put on weight easily. He wanted him fatter and fatter, so keen was he on money. "As long as they put a hefty ring through his nose and cover his eyes with a sack, the handlers will easily be the boss of him," he said.

    Hermine felt sorry for the animal, especially because of his dismal prospects. It was Saturday evening; she went into the barn. She was playing and found herself beyond the cow in front, who had already settled down for the night. They were all lying down; only the bull still stood. So they had given him too much to eat again. Hermine was in a good and helpful state of mind: she had made her confession that afternoon, and the next day she was supposed to take communion. She stroked, she comforted. To this day Hermine doesn't know exactly what came over her. By way of excuse she can only say that the bull helped her to do it. He stretched out his muzzle, made it thin, and while she was petting, the end bit of the chain slipped through the ring. The clang of the falling chains frightened her right away. She wanted to undo the deed, make it not have happened. She took fright especially at the happy demeanor of the bull. He tried to lick her face, shook his giant head for joy and made playful leaps.

Tell Father? But she was afraid of her father. She looked for the hired hand. For back then they still had one, even if he didn't amount to much. He was deaf and dumb. Therefore on Sunday he got four marks from Father, instead of seven. Mother said all the same he was a hard worker, and scolded the children: "You mustn't laugh at him, when he's trying to say something and can't get it out." In the end Hermine talked herself into thinking that Thomas wouldn't have understood her anyway. And now, what a bad night she had! True, Hermine heard nothing from the barn; all the same she was scared of what she might hear, and tossed and turned. She knew it and felt it: what she'd done with the chain was a sin against the fourth commandment. If she took communion like that, it would be a deadly sin. If she simply stayed away, everyone would ask where she'd been. Finally she found the solution. She would make her confession again, before early mass. People would look at her strangely, for only men went to confession then, men who really had no time for it on Saturday, or who had sinned anew in the night. Very early the next morning she came into the kitchen.

Mother was bossy with her: "It's way too early, and you're not getting anything to eat." But Hermine knew this already: before you went, you mustn't let a single crumb pass your lips. She wanted to wash. The only running water in the house was in use. Father was shaving. Waiting for him, Hermine watched and listened. It was a nice noise, when he scraped out of his face a week of stubble. Father's skin came out faultless from underneath the foam. She was tempted to confess to him, but the sharp razor in his hand held her back. And anyway she was just thinking that only the priest had the authority to forgive sins—when Thomas burst into the kitchen, fighting for words. "P-p-p-priest's gone!" That's what it sounded like, and Hermine almost felt lighter in her heart. But then they were running towards the barn, and she realized that Thomas had used the strange word *beast* for the bull. And, yes, the bull was gone. The thick neck chain was broken in two, and the head chain must have come loose by itself. That's what Father said, and they had to leave everything just as it was, so others could see that the bull had been chained up three ways, in case anything happened.

It was summer. The upper wing of the barn door stood open; the lower had been splintered at its edge. Armed with stiletto and club, father went out in the road, to warn the neighbors everywhere on their way to church and to fetch the ranger and the butcher. Mother asked the children to pray for their father. That made everything more terrible yet.

As the men stood around the farmyard talking over their plans for the hunt, the bull came trotting out of the woods and down the road. The hunters moved up the slope that bordered the roadside, to get a better view. Everyone who was in the house ran up the winding stair to the windows on the upper floor. The bull trotted along at his ease. Outdoors he didn't look as gigantic as he had in the barn. Where the road turned into the farmyard, he stood still. Hermine was amazed that he knew where he lived. He seemed to be thinking it over, whether it was really a good idea to go back home at all. The butcher, or rather Weisshaupt, since this was a Sunday, stuck the big knife back in his wooden knifecase. He reached for a stick instead. "This is the way to get him into the barn," he said. Thomas came out of the barn with a prod, meaning to leave the bull no choice. "Thomas! Thomas!" He didn't hear the outcry; he only heard people when he could see their mouths. Now he was looking at the bull. The bull let him come quite close; then he charged. Thomas ran for his pitiful life. He would have been lost if he hadn't delivered himself to the top of the high-stacked hay wagon in front of the barn door. No one would have guessed he could run and climb so fast. The furious bull struck the wagon boards with his horns. He tossed tufts of grass around him. The gamekeeper aimed. Father cried: "Don't!"; for he still had hopes for his own great shot. Suddenly the bull let out a dreadful bellow at Thomas. Then he ran out of the farmyard, back towards the woods whence he had come. No way they would let him get that far.

How it all ended, Hermine didn't get to see. But the men told the story so often she felt she had been there: saw how the ranger had had to shoot again and again, at close range. Saw above all, in exact detail, the dance of death that the bull had done, for he had turned in circles a good ten times before he fell and finally received the knife. They had more trouble with the horse; it shied as they put it to harness before the bloody beast. Only when it came clattering half crazed into the barnyard with its strange burden could Hermine be free of her own unbearable tension. Until that moment she had feared that the bull might give her away.

Only a couple of the most pious got to church. They came in after communion, and still it was a fair trade to endure the dumb stares of the other churchgoers, if they themselves could be first with the news.

Then they had to get Schorpin. She lived in the next village over and had two callings. She was either the death-cryer or the meat-cryer; as the death-cryer she went from farmhouse to farmhouse and said, "Locher from Vorderreute bids you come, whoever will, to pray at eight in the evening and, whoever will, on Thursday at half past nine to the burial, leaving the house at nine, the grandmother is dead." She said this very fast, in falsetto, exactly the same speech in every case, except for the names and dates. Should you ask what had ailed the grandmother, she would tell you in her deep, calm voice of the departed's last hour: say, that she was already dead when the priest came, but he gave her last rites all the same. For this Schorpin got an egg, a chunk of bread and a God-bless-you. That was her living.

When she was meat-cryer, her little speech was almost the same: This or that farmer bids you come, whoever will, only in this case at a certain hour you could get meat, sixty *pfennig* a pound. The usual question—what had ailed the cow, for it followed from that whether five pounds might be bought, or only two—they could skip this time. The story of the bull had already come out in the newspaper, under the headline "Buffalo Hunt." The meat went fast. The bad bull made a good soup. Even days later people were coming to ask if they didn't have any more to sell. Father almost lost his reason for vexation. He reckoned it up, again and again, how much he'd have saved off the top at seventy *pfennig* a pound instead of sixty, or if he'd only been able to sell the bull in the normal way. It was a bitter time. And most of all for Hermine. It's true she was able to go to confession the following Saturday. It didn't attract attention; no one would go to communion with a week's weight of new sin.

But confession brought her no peace. Just the opposite: the priest said that undoing the chain had been no sin. She hadn't done it to make mischief, but rather out of pity for the beast. Next time she should ask her father first—and he gave her, for her other sins, a laughable penance. The priest knew nothing about anything! Nothing of her father and nothing about animals on a farm. On the front steps of the church, terror seized her. If it was no sin, then it was not covered by the confidentiality of the confessional. The priest might tell anyone; and with that began Hermine's grimmest days. Of course she dared not irritate the priest. She learned the catechism questions to a hair, and read the Bible stories in advance so that she could retell them all as if she had been there herself. The priest praised her. That terrified her all over again. She must not attract his attention too much, otherwise he might well praise her great love of animals. She gave wrong answers sometimes, even though she knew the right ones, which wasn't easy. But it was worse yet whenever Father went into town and came back again. Hermine eyed him: what kind of face was he making? Did he know yet? Sometimes she wished he would just let loose and beat her half dead, and there would be an end to it.

It was a long time before it did end. How bad "the bad bull" really was—for he went down in history under that name—came out only months later. All the cows who weren't then in calf, but who were ready to be so, became so, in that one night. Even the cow at the far back of the row, who was actually still a calf herself, he managed to mount before he made his great leap into the open. That cow was simply too young to carry the devil's seed to term. When Schorpin told them, in her normal voice, that they had to slaughter her because of trouble with the calf, people resolved to take no meat. Only kinfolks, and near neighbors, shamefacedly bought a couple of pounds. For such animals are in great pain, and feverish. That makes the meat sweet. It was in warm springtime. When they had finally eaten up all that meat, they wanted only chopped pancakes, sauerkraut noodles, or cheese spätzle, even on the finest Sunday.

For her resurrection Hermine actually had a cousin to thank who lived in the same village, quite near them. He stuck a tobacco pipe in the back of his pants while it was still burning, and she saw the smoke. Therefore she had saved him from a fiery death. In return, she was allowed to visit his place. For it was known that this cousin had no liking for little girls. When they got too close to him he would say, "I'll turn your blood red all right," or "I'll make your ears stand on end." To Hermine he said these terrible things no more. She could hang around him and eavesdrop. The cousin had a wise remark for every perplexing human situation. Thus she heard him say, "Every week a new cow runs through the village," or, "Time heals all wounds." Once he even said, "The grass grows over every misdeed." And on that note Hermine slowly came to herself again. At about this time the good priest, to Hermine's great relief, went to his last reward.

Horse

Some days Hermine liked well enough. Not Christmas. Then she felt sick half the time from the rich cookies. And while some of her sisters and brothers were good singers, this talent had skipped over her completely. At most they could ask Hermine how the fourth verse went. Before the caroling started on Christmas Eve, Mother said to her: "But you best keep quiet." Somehow that put Hermine in a sad mood every year.

She liked Shrovetide, especially the days just after carnival eve. Ash Wednesday was out and out her happiest day, for that was the one day of the year when her father thought well of her. Mother cooked a kettle full of stockfish. She herself ate no more than would fit on the end of a fork, just enough so father could tell she wasn't trying to poison him. He and Hermine, between the two of them, cleaned the bowl. She was allowed to sit next to him, and they looked down on the others with their porridge, which some of them ate shiny with fat on top, others with sugar and cinnamon. To Hermine the flaky white meat of stockfish looked alluring. She even liked the taste of it, and for that she soared in her father's esteem. Besides all that, she was partial to the season. Spring wasn't there yet, but it hung in the air. That made her gay every year, even giddy. On *Funkensonntag* her mood rose to the point of wildness. She always felt well then; the

Spark Sunday wreaths that her mother baked were made of plain yeast dough. And so when the sparks of the bonfire flew, she too skipped and squealed. Sometimes they really had to speak to her. Every year she was one of the last to leave the smoking ash heap.

Sadly, one Spark Sunday went off quite another way. The day began as usual; the Sunday was even especially fine. Easter must have come late that year, for spring no longer hung in the air; it was there. And the brush pile up on the hill was big, the witch magnificent. At four the older children started home to supper and chores in the barn, so that they would have plenty of time for the merry evening ahead. As they did every year, the little ones pulled long switches from the bonfire heap, to beat the snow with them. That was a particular custom in that little village. Usually snow lay close by, but this year they had to look for it. Finally they found a patch of white on the north slope of the old gravel quarry. That snow had to do heavy penance for being the last. The children whipped, the snow spurted, they yelled and screamed, the echoes carried far.

Now, the farmer from the second farm into the village was a fool for horses. He bought, he sold; plenty of times he even had a useless third horse in the stall. Hermine's father, who had the same Max and Moritz his whole life long, used to say, "Furtler will do himself out of house and home with those ponies." All the same, Furtler understood horses. He knew that they mustn't stand idle in the barn all day. He was taking his prize nag for a walk. The horse shied at the screaming of the children and ran off. As if witches were after it, it galloped down the road. The road made a sharp curve. Right there the first farmer into the village had his garden fence. For three colored glass balls, a few radishes and some asters that bloomed in the fall, it was a fearsome enclosure. So many sharp-pointed, rusty iron spears, every three feet a higher one, and those at the corner of the garden higher yet, with curved barbs.

The horse couldn't make the curve, and spitted himself. His screams rang out so that all the village ran to the spot; even the watchmen from the brush pile came running. The men brought beams to lever the horse up with. This took time, for they were getting a beating from the animal's hooves. And he was heavy besides. When they had finally managed it and set the horse on the road, he fell over as if pushed, laid his beautiful head far away from the dreadful wound, and died.

They wanted to say it was Hermine's fault. And they did say that for sure she had screamed the loudest. She was crying so hard that she had no voice to tell them it wasn't true. And anyway she knew it was true.

Suddenly someone cried: "The bonfire!" In late afternoon it was blazing away. Even as they watched, the burning witch fell over. They comforted each other, saying they couldn't have had much fun anyway. Only Hermine talked one younger sister into going up the hill with her once it was dark. For she really thought she couldn't bear it. Up there it still smoked and stank. They saw the *Funkensonntag* bonfires of the Forderreuters and the Schwarzenbachers, and they knew which town each fire belonged to. From the village nearest them they heard music and noise, and Hermine had never been so sad.

The following Sunday, the new priest thundered down at them from the pulpit. On *Funkensonntag* he had either heard some particularly wild goings-on himself, or someone had reported back to him and wildly exaggerated. "There was even dancing!" This the priest cried out in a mighty voice. "And that on a Lenten Sunday! As the suffering of Our Lord is beginning! Wilt thou backslide into heathenry?" He went on like that for a full half hour. Those from the sinful village looked at the floor. Those from the unlucky village smirked at each other. Their conscience was clear, and they didn't begrudge the others the angry sermon, since they had found out in the meanwhile who had set their *Funkensonntag* pile on fire. But the last part of that sermon lay like a hundredweight on Hermine's soul. The joy of pulling pranks, the joy of spring, the last bit of the joy of life went out of it for her. For the priest had thundered down that they must always keep that true saying in mind: "As your Sunday goes, so goes the day of your death." Now, Hermine knew about bad Sundays, and sad Sundays, and Sundays full of dread; she even knew how, when bad luck happened to her on a Saturday, on Sunday she still suffered from it. For a long time after, the thought of the hour of her death never left her, for if what the priest said was true, then that was sure to bring her the worst luck of all.

Dog

Twice a week a knitting teacher came to their school. Her real name was Josefine, but all the world called her Seff-e-le. She taught the girls knitting and crocheting, which they knew how to do already. These were little girls up to fourth grade on the one afternoon, and big girls from the upper three grades on the other. The rest of the time Seffele was a seamstress who worked house to house, making the finest Sunday dresses for would-be fine ladies and their daughters. For men's shirts there was another seamstress thereabouts. Seffele had a dainty look about her, delicate and refined with little brown curls. The girls in the highest class wondered why she hadn't got a husband yet. At that time, in her first school year, Hermine was completely infatuated with Seffele, her person and all she did and said. She let it be known to all that some day she wanted to be just like Seffele.

Seffele was not only pretty herself, she had a pretty little house too. It was a bit farther away from the schoolhouse than Kitz's place and had a small shed built on. Her dead father had once been warder of roads. In one corner of the little added-on room stood the attributes of the sainted one: a scruffy broom, a shovel, and a peculiar sort of wheelbarrow like no one else's. Seffele set up these objects to his blessed memory, and the children stood before them as at a shrine. For they used to come into Seffele's little shed on their way home from school, to throw their schoolbags in a far corner of it. They had a long walk home. But they couldn't always get away with leaving their schoolbags at Seffele's. They had to have no homework, or so little they could do it quickly by the side of the road. And, besides, the door had to be open, and sometimes it was locked. The children never completely saw through the reason for that; just that it was bound up with the schoolmaster somehow. Seffele was seldom at home, but when she was, the children didn't need to rattle the latch to know whether or not her door was locked. They could tell from far away by Seffele's dog. If the door was locked, he ran around barking and showing his teeth. But if it was open, he lay sullenly on the stoop and only growled at them when they tossed in their schoolbags. When Seffele was at other people's houses, he lay under her worktable all day long, even let himself be covered with bits of fabric. When Seffele was at school, he lay in a hole under the schoolhouse steps and never moved. He was fat, ugly and ill-natured. He didn't like the children, and they didn't like him either.

Now, Seffele had the God-given gift that every creature did her bidding. The girls listened to Seffele's every word. They were nearly as obedient as the dog. Their mothers likewise had to obey and buy exactly the wool that Seffele specified, even when they didn't have the money. And most of all, the schoolteacher and the priest had to obey. They disposed their free afternoons according to Seffele's wishes. For their name days she collected money and bought the presents and designed the festivities after her own fine notions. And then even the little boys had to obey. Maybe that was how it had come about that she had no husband. Everybody's Sunday dresses in the place had the same collars, buttons and belt buckles, as ordained from above by Seffele. If any of them went their own way, she was terribly put out.

Hermine had a friend, a girl with snow-white hair and skin so rosy pink she seemed to have come straight from her bath. And pretty Luzia was allowed to be nursemaid at the teacher's house—that is, she looked after his children. One day the homework was piling up mightily: even before mid-morning recess the teacher had assigned so many long-divisions-with-proofs that they were afraid they would run out of space on the back sides of their slates. By eleven the word-family for "to fare" had been added, and just before the end of school, a short reading to be retold later in your own words, on top of that. So today it would be all the same to them whether Seffele's door was open or not. As they were packing up their bookbags, the schoolmaster said to Luzia, who shared a desk with Hermine: "Come over right after dinner. You needn't do any homework today." Hermine blinked at him. For practically every day the schoolmaster made a point of saying that he was fair and made no exceptions. So now he began to praise Hermine and Luzia: these two, Hermine and also Luzia, were his very best pupils. It was only fair that he reward them for once and excuse them from their homework. And somehow, the way he said it, it sounded as if Luzia had Hermine to thank for it. So the two of them had all the luck: they could leave their bags at Seffele's, and the others were envious.

The next morning, Seffele's door didn't seem to be shut, but for some reason the dog stood in front of it and bared his teeth. And all at once Hermine and Luzia recalled that today was the memorial mass for Seffele's father. True, the man was already ten years dead. But since it was Seffele's father, he would still be remembered by name from the pulpit. They had completely forgotten about it. Of course the dog wasn't allowed in the church. So he stood there, offering to tear them both to pieces. On the path their schoolfellows laughed; they had their bags, so they would get to school on time. Hermine and Luzia picked up sticks and stones and ran in mounting despair around the little house. Whatever was keeping her? But who knew how long she'd stand there at the grave, until everyone saw how deeply she still grieved! Suddenly the dog tucked his tail between his legs. The way to the schoolbags lay open. In the distance they saw Seffele, dressed all in black.

Pure gloating beamed out at them from the schoolroom: the two model schoolgirls were very late. The schoolmaster was in a bad humor; wherever he had gone the day before, he must not have enjoyed himself. Hermine and Luzia were condemned to two strokes each, across the hand, with the cane. These were the first they had ever gotten. Luzia's turn came first. Hermine's fear drained away. The strokes were feeble; Hermine saw that she cried only for shame. But when her own strokes came, the cane whistled in the air. They were—in the language of the initiated—juicy ones. In fact the teacher threw his fine principles entirely to the wind. He gave it to Hermine two extra times, now left, now right, the cane whistling ever louder. For it happened that, between Luzia's strokes and Hermine's, the teacher had asked whether Fraülein Jehle knew the girls dumped their schoolbags in her shed. Lying suited neither Luzia's honor as nursemaid nor her pale skin. So it was Hermine who said: "Seffele has no idea." That was false—as all three of them knew. She should have told the truth—that sometimes it was open, at other times locked up tight. When he gave her the extra strokes, Hermine had the queer feeling that they were not for her but for Seffele, who had no idea about anything.

Cows

"She's too stupid to mind cows. Send her off to school," cursed Father. Hermine fought back: it was the cows' fault. But Father shouted: "Already last year and the year before you couldn't be the boss of them." As pleasant as it was to tend the cows in company with her sisters and brothers, so was it dismal when the others had some real work to do and Hermine was left alone with the herd. Right away the cows started in to torment her. Three ran into the neighbor's beet field. That couldn't be allowed, for in the least little time they would lay it most dreadfully to waste. She ran quick to stop them. But then two others were already at the fruit trees. That was even worse. The smallest apple accidentally swallowed down could be the death of a cow. And so Hermine left one cow to rampage in the beets for the time being, while she chased the others away from the ruinous apples.

But they had at the time one old cow who, whenever she was in the barn, would start bawling and pushing already at eleven, so eager was she to get out. But as soon as she had stilled the worst of her hunger pangs outside, she wanted back in the barn again. When she saw that no cowherd stood in front of her, she took off running towards home. Now Hermine had a real emergency on her hands. She had to drop all the other urgent defensive measures and run with all her strength to cut off the old cow along the way. But the cow had already hoisted her tail high, her long udder slapped up against her back as she galloped, and she was ready to run Hermine over. In the meantime the despoilers of the beets and the plunderers of the apples had noticed what was up. They didn't actually care to go home just yet, but neither did they want to miss the fun. So they too raised their tails high and thundered homewards like a barbarian horde. This, now, was the worst of all. Father was furious. If it was still early in the afternoon, either he had to start all over again and drive the cows back out to pasture, or, if this no longer seemed worth the trouble, then he must dip into his precious hay supply. All this and more like it had happened to Hermine again and again; this year, last year, and—just as father had scolded—already the year before that.

Girl

Hare

Hermine had far to go to her school in the city. One evening when she came home, they all sat at table in the dusk; they were saving electricity. Hermine went to throw her schoolbag where it belonged, after a long day at school. On her third step towards the dark corner came a pitiful squeak from underfoot. Working in the field that day, they had caught a little hare. It must have been a pretty one, for now they set upon Hermine without mercy. She was deeply sorry for the accident, and said so. One sister had just come from the nearest town, where she had bought a little bottle with a nipple, since they themselves had no more little ones about the place. "All for nothing on account of blind-as-a-bat! Money thrown away because of the clod!" Those were some of the names they called her. For once, however, Father came to Hermine's aid. "Nobody has ever yet succeeded in raising a wild hare from a baby." Hermine knew, of course, that he took her part mainly because now the hare would drink up no more milk. All the same she was grateful to him.

Cat

With cats Hermine had no luck. She had taken a wonderful book out of the school library: Hans and Eva wanted to get married. But far and wide there was no priest to be found, and also not the faintest hope of getting to a church. Hermine found this thrilling, and she tried to read on at the supper table. Father was not pleased. As punishment she had to clear the table. Then she made sloppy work of it. She didn't put the milk jug—it was a white enamel basin that narrowed dramatically on top—back in the kitchen cupboard; in fact, she didn't cover it at all, but hurried back to her book.

Then just as she was getting annoyed at the writer for going off on one irrelevant tangent after another, there came a fearful noise from the kitchen, as if every cooking tin in the place had been hurled against the wall. What had happened was worse yet. The cat had the milk jug over its head like a hat and was tearing blindly about. Hermine's quick sister paid the deep scratches she got no mind, and grabbed the animal. Father pulled at the jug. Mother poured on salad oil, so that the cat's head would slide. One brother tried to widen the mouth of the jug with a hammer. Nothing worked. A tin shear!—Hermine offered to ride a bicycle to the plumber's. Father roared: "Stay where you are!" For by now the cat was making peculiar twitches. Father decided to end her suffering and broke her spine with one hard blow. Then he raised the same hammer at Hermine. "I ought to . . ." He spoke to her no more after that—just the essentials.

Bat

It was summer, Sunday evening. They sat out long on the front step of the house. The pale sandstone was still warm from the sun. They sang. They could do that, sing in fine two-part harmony; Hermine they asked how the third verse started. They sang about the fairest meadowland and the elderberry bush, about the two friends who went ever in the same step—everything that fit, they sang about. Gradually they began, one after the other, to go to bed, for they all had their tasks the next day. One brother was a moralist. Though he knew that Hermine had her tasks too, he knew as well that she couldn't say no, so he told her to stay there on the stoop and tell him later who her big sister came home with.

At first it was lovely for her, all alone on the steps with the front door open at her back. It was quite still. Crickets were chirping. Frogs croaked up from the pond. A fine mist lay on the meadow, and over the big apple tree hung the moon. Where they lived the land was always beautiful, in rain and sunshine, in summer as in winter, by day and by night. Hermine undid her braids, the quicker to get to bed afterwards. Her hair wasn't curly anymore, but so thick that an animal could lose its way in it. And now one did in fact fly at her head and lose its way. It squeaked, whistled and sent out shrill screams. Both of them beat about wildly. Then it bit Hermine in her left ear. Now she screamed too. Attracted by all this screaming, her moral brother arrived and freed her from the animal. Full of disgust he flung it against the steps. They stared at it, horrified. Ugly as the devil's smallest child it sat there, showed its many needle-sharp teeth, cheeped, squealed and foamed at the mouth. Hermine was deeply ashamed in front of her brother, to have had something so ugly in her hair. She even wept for shame, but just said that her ear hurt. Finally the furious bat spread its great naked wings out and flew away.

Buck

Every summer a boy was sent to her uncle's farm on holiday. Bit by bit he grew into a tall, good-looking youth. Most of the time he hung about their place, probably because of all the girls. Every one of the girls was looking for her chance with him. Hermine, too, but on her he wasted scarcely a glance. She made up her mind to do something about that. She knew a good spot in the woods for strawberry-picking. One evening she took him along. She promised him a lot of strawberries and even carried his pail for him. It was a fine night. The day before, it had rained, and the strawberry patch teemed with berries, more even than Hermine had dared to hope. Anyone who has ever found berries in such a place knows what greed overtakes the picker. The little berries aren't good enough anymore. There, that way, ever bigger red dots beckon. Now the holiday boy was seized with strawberry fever too. Hermine was in bliss to think she'd been able to give him this pleasure. The pails were nearly full. Still they couldn't stop themselves, although in the meantime dusk had deepened in the woods. Suddenly a buck roared in the thicket quite near them. Or he bayed, or bellowed. It scared them. The young man dropped his pail. They ran away wildly. Afterwards the boy didn't want his berries back. They had scooped them up in such haste that now there were twigs and grass blades among them. Hermine offered him hers, but now he was having none of it, or her.

Fox

The little village was crammed full of soldiers on maneuvers. Her big sister passed on to Hermine the office of shutting up the chicken coop. She favored Hermine, because Hermine, thanks to the bat, hadn't betrayed her and, besides, would be leaving home the day after next, on Monday, to go on with her schooling. The sister was going to the Maneuver Ball. She gave Hermine exact instructions. To wit, there were four hens who preferred to spend the night in the tree instead of in the chicken coop. Only when these had been brought to order might the coop be fastened. In her zeal, Hermine poked at them a little too early. The chickens flew stubbornly back to their branch. When the whole thing repeated itself and after more prodding the chickens still acted as if they didn't know where the henhouse was, Hermine had no choice but to wait for the twilight to darken. Meanwhile in the front yard of the farmhouse a hot dodgeball match was raging, between civilians and military. They were glad when Hermine came on, as reinforcement, to the civilian side, for the contest was dogged as well as merry. Victory and defeat went back and forth. On the military side there were six young warriors who would rather play ball than dance. At last the ball flew into the vegetable garden, where on account of the deepening dark it could no longer be found. They fooled around for a long while yet in the farmyard, and Hermine liked that. Finally Father up in his bedroom had had enough, and chased the whole company to bed.

So how was it that her sister, coming home at midnight, had other things in her head than the chicken coop? The fox had made a clever job of it. Neither dog nor human noticed anything, although the chicken coop lay between their two houses. The soldiers could have learned a lot from the fox, most of all about nocturnal combat. The contest was unequal: one against thirty, and the fox won. Only four hens were left over; these sat there in the morning stunned and goggle-eyed up in their tree. For all the others it must be allowed that they are stupid, while the fox is sly; he is a night hunter, while they are night-blind. "There must have been two foxes," a lot of people speculated. Whatever else went on, dawn must have sorely pressed the fox in the end, for his last opponents he no longer dragged to his den, but buried them instead in the vegetable garden, whose little gate had been left open on account of the lost ball. Crooked hen's legs, blood and feathers stuck up out of the garden beds.

They hated Hermine more than they hated the fox. She was glad that she could flee her home. Mother usually built up her children's strength with fried eggs when they were going away. Hermine had to march off into the unknown with undunked bread and jam in her stomach.

Spider

Hermine was being educated in the city. Here she had no more to do with animals—only the usual vermin. The schoolgirls had to be introduced to good literature. To that end they were to practice reading aloud. Every week three Literary Evenings were scheduled. The German teacher was invariably present. Beyond pure zeal, the girls suspected her of a certain sadism, since out of all the beauties of German literature she chose only those stories that had something gruesome in them: "A Night in the Hunting Lodge," or "The Jew's Beech." And it amazed them how many she could find. Hermine was to read out loud from "The Black Spider," by Jeremias Gotthelf. This wouldn't be easy, said the teacher, but Hermine's Upper Swabian dialect shouldn't make a bad match with the Swiss story. Hermine tried her best. But again and again she was interrupted by storms of laughter. It seemed that not even in dear old Switzerland in the good old days could Upper Swabian be understood. Hermine's schoolfellows came from Stuttgart, from Tübingen, even from as far away as Balingen. Everyone was used to their citified High German, and it was universally admired. But not only for the sake of her pronunciation did Hermine torture herself for two whole weeks with that spider. She was hearing, to say nothing of reading, about the black spider for the first time. She would lose her breath. Her voice grew smaller and smaller and deserted her altogether. Then tears welled up and she couldn't read on. The teacher scolded. It was certainly praiseworthy, she said, when the reader partook of the meaning of what she read; but this was going too far. Only when the hideous spider was at last stuck fast in its bung-hole could she bring the story more or less smoothly to its close.

Her roommate was assigned to read "Under the Pear Tree," by Fontane. She brought it off swimmingly. Hermine knew that the Pole buried in the cellar would have given her far less trouble than the diabolical spider, and would have earned her at least as good a mark. Hermine's old teacher at home, who asked to see her first report card, was deeply disappointed in her German grade. "But you always wrote such fine little essays," he said unhappily, and never asked to see her report card again.

Mosquitoes

Over three years she got to stay in that school. The last summer was a hot summer in wartime. Beside the big house lay a lovely park with an ornamental pond in it, a regular breeding farm for mosquitoes. By night thousands of mosquitoes invaded the open windows—for closed windows would have been too much to bear—and fell upon the innocently sleeping girls. It was strictly forbidden, however, to strike so much as one mosquito dead against the wall. Such a stain from a mosquito cost a fine of twenty *pfennig*; that was a lot of money back then.

In the city there was also a lazaret, a hospital for wounded soldiers, for longer convalescences, until they were completely recovered. And now the head office of the girls' school had the idea of holding a summer-night's fest for these hard-stricken men. They had to wait for a night with a full moon, for they were not allowed to burn lights at that time. The teachers instructed the girls to be friendly to their soldier guests after the performances, to ask them, say, in which theater of the war they had been wounded or where their homes were. One "course" held theatricals, another sang songs, yet another danced folk dances, and select groups performed gymnastic drills to perfection. The guests were delighted. Some events had to be repeated, because of all the applause. Meanwhile it had gotten late. The headmistress said it was high time now for the girls to be in bed. Hermine and the girl she shared her room with liked to go back by roundabout ways. Along one such out-of-the-way path sat a soldier, on a bench. It seemed he hadn't watched any of the entertainments. Both girls were frightened, for the man had no hair. They wanted to pass quickly by, but he said to them pleadingly, or rather urgently, in a beautiful voice: "Sit down with me, won't you please, I have something to tell you." They couldn't refuse. He pointed to the full moon and said, almost sang, the old nursery rhyme: "The moon is round. *Der Mond ist rund, der Mond ist rund, er hat zwei Augen, Nase, Mund.*" And at the same time he drew on the sky: circle, points, line; like a little child, drew a face with two eyes, nose, mouth; and did this again and again.

Hermine's roommate asked, according to their instructions, where he had been wounded. He said absently: "In the head." And then he began to tell a story. Probably it was meant to be a memory of the war, yet the sentences lacked all connection. But they were beautiful sentences, all alone as they stood there. Hermine listened as if under a spell. Then they wanted to go, but he held Hermine's hand fast and begged: "Oh but please stay! I really have something to tell you." And again he began: "The moon is round . . ." Hermine's roommate laughed and ran away. What he said after that had to do with his sister, but made no sense even so. Hermine asked where his home was. "In Dresden." He talked on, about mountains. She saw that his head was not completely bald. It had a kind of baby down on it. His face was handsome; most of all Hermine liked his dark, sad, good-natured eyes. Despite all that, Hermine now had to go. Her door and his gate, she said, would otherwise be locked. She pointed out, for him, where he could find the shortest path to the gate. She had gone only the littlest bit of the way when he came running after her. "He wants to say goodnight again or even to give me a kiss," thought Hermine. But he seized her by the hand and drew her excitedly after him, said he had something to say to her. He pulled her as far as the pond. There lay the full moon in reflection, and he drew its outline above the water, while he sang: "The moon . . ."

On the lawn where they had had their entertainments there still sat a couple of woman teachers with officers. Hermine crept by. Luckily the door was still open. Inside, at the entrance to the staircase, stood the porter. There's one like him in almost every school: he nursed some kind of grudge against the students. Now if he had just shouted at her, Hermine would have liked that a good deal better than his malevolent laugh. He showed up the next day during midday rest with the teacher who had charge of order in the house. This woman was a dragon, in looks and manner. But Hermine's roommate could talk. She stood by Hermine: It had just been a poor madman, she said, who had pressed them pitifully to listen to him. The porter observed to his chagrin that the storm in a teacup was blowing over. But then he saw them, to his joy: mosquito stains on the wall. In the confusion of the night gone by, and in need of sleep that wouldn't come, Hermine had broken the commandment and slapped a few times with a used-up copy-book against the wallpaper. Along with the new spots, the housemaster counted up ancient stains, marks of Hermine's predecessors, stains that had already been paid for once before. The total fine outstripped Hermine's scanty monthly pocket money by a long way. Now she had to keep her violence within bounds and pay off what she owed in installments over several months. So Hermine never got to see the wonderful film about the city of gold.

Then there came another full moon. Hermine accompanied her classmates as far as the cashier's window of the movie house. *Ride for Germany* was being shown just then. It wasn't yet dark when she chose the roundabout way home, by the lazaret. A few men were there, sitting or standing around in the park. She would have liked to see him again. Maybe his hair had grown in thicker in the meantime? And what if he should speak to her? Maybe the sentences he said would hang together by now. But she didn't see him.

When she lay in her bed, patiently bearing the hum of the mosquitoes and their bites, the full moon stood in the window. "The moon is . . ." She was on the point of mimicking him. Then she thought: "Maybe he's already up there, with his moon." Suddenly it was like a certainty in her, that, even if he weren't so already, rather sooner than later, he would be with the moon in still water.

Swallow

The old teacher had a new teacher at his side. The energetic young teacher organized a village festival at the beginning of summer vacation. Hermine's younger sisters and brothers, who were still going to school, all had something to do at the fest. Father got a special invitation; Mother, too, of course. They were all putting on their best for the evening. Hermine had hurried home in time for the holiday. She donned her new summer dress, expecting to be included in the festivities. "You aren't coming," her father said to her. It was a bitter disappointment for Hermine. She would have liked to see for herself the "fabulous" young teacher. She had even hoped that he might have something to say to her, since she was training for the same honorable calling as his own. Although Father saw the disappointment in Hermine's face, he didn't back down from his order. He probably wouldn't have begrudged her the pleasure, but her joy was outweighed by his oppressive sense that there were just too many of them. He was forever embarrassed at the number of his children.

Just as he was heading down the front stoop, a swallow flew over him and let something drop on his shoulder. The blotch was large and looked disgusting on Father's Sunday suit. They all trooped back again, while Mother got Father cleaned up.

Hermine stood nearby and perhaps a shade of gloating passed over her face. In fury at her, or at his mishap, Father threw a fist at her and caught her on the forehead. She saw little stars. She sat herself down on the bench behind the house and wept noisily. Suddenly Father stood before her and said she could go with them after all. "I don't want to anymore," said Hermine. Now Father lost control of his temper completely. He beat Hermine, left and right about the face and everywhere that he could reach. His hand was hard—Hermine not quite eighteen years old. Later, half insensible, she fell into bed.

The village festival was a success, and next day her sisters and brothers were in fine spirits. Father kept clear of Hermine. Mother said to her: "It was a nice celebration, but I couldn't get in the mood for it. I couldn't stop thinking of you. The young teacher even asked about you and said someone should fetch you. But your father had given you that awful beating on account of the swallow." And after a while she said again: "Yes, you'd have felt right at home at that sort of affair."

Mole Cricket

On her short spring break Hermine brought lots of books home to study. But then she liked it better to go off to the fields with her sisters to cut thistles. They went along the meadow just far enough from one another so they could keep on talking, and struck the heads off the young thistles with the sharp little blades at the ends of their long poles. Too bad Father soon came to collect the sisters who knew what they were doing about the farm and give them some proper work.

Hermine was alone in the great field, with no end in sight to the dull job before her. Meanwhile the day grew hot and close. She deeply regretted that she hadn't told them she had to study. And there was something worse. Although she was going on eighteen, only last night for the first time had it come, that flow that a change of air and landscape had so long held off—now that she was back in the circle of home. With every thrust her whole body hurt, until she thought she couldn't stand it anymore. And so she lay down on the edge of the field and fell asleep. Soon a cool tickle on her upper arm awakened her. "It's just a blade of grass," she thought, and didn't bother to open her weary eyes. Only when it started to hurt, she looked. And then with a cry of horror she jumped up and flung it from her, what she had seen on her naked arm. It was a pair of mole crickets—

horse-biters, children called them, and traded stories about them, how ten of them could kill a horse. Hermine had always considered that an old-wives'-tale. Why should exactly ten of them come together and bite a horse to death? Nor had these two meant to bite Hermine. She suspected that they'd had something less respectable in mind, especially since there'd been the two of them and they had stood one in back of the other so peculiarly. Probably it was in expectation of some sort of fit of passion from the one behind that the one in front had stuck itself fast to Hermine's skin. Now her repulsion was complete. These were creatures of abysmal ugliness, and for a long time, even after her return to school, Hermine shuddered to think she'd had something so disgusting on her bare skin, and so close before her eyes.

Miss

Bear

Hermine was now a teacher—she was a *Miss*, and had her first post. At the end of gym period, she liked to play a lively game with the children. She was always looking for fresh ones. A game from her childhood came back to her. Upon the cry, *Bear out of the hole!,* the whole group ran by one child lurking in a corner. This one captured helpers out of every wave that went by, until one last runner was left over as the new bear. Two children still had to run past the dangerous horde of bears: one small and quick little fellow, and a girl. That girl had a boundless will to win. Her brown eyes shone, her cheeks burned, her black curls flew behind her. Hermine trembled for the excited, plump little she-bear, who never noticed that the boy had already been caught; she rushed on, too far, until her head struck the wall. And there she lay unconscious. And stayed that way much too long. Hermine never found out if the girl was ever so wild again after that. She received her reprimand: gym is no place for a bear hunt. She was transferred.

May Beetles

Now she came to teach in a large village that lay in a pretty valley. This place was famous for its cherries; they flourished there. When Hermine arrived, they had already been eaten up for that year. The war was still on. The teachers and their classes were being misused in every possible way: scouring the potato fields for nonexistent beetles, plucking flax, gathering beechnuts, hunting for wood and pinecones in the forest so that in winter the school needn't close down quite so often.

Then in the spring trouble came down on Hermine on account of the May beetles. It was a terrible year for *Maikäfer*. The oaks and beeches were as bare again as in winter. People were afraid the same would happen to the cherry trees. Every morning early, the teachers along with their children had to report for duty with the farmers—Hermine, as it happened, at the town hall, for the town too owned rows of cherry trees. Here was no farmer who had brought along a ladder for the work; instead two prisoners, two Frenchmen, were standing there. The children got old paper sacks and buckets. Hermine took a bucket too. The Frenchmen had to climb the trees without a ladder and shake the branches with all their strength. The night-dazed beetles crackled. Hermine and the children picked them up.

One Frenchman was young and handsome, with

wonderful teeth and shining black eyes. While the other one waited, leaning sullenly against the tree trunk, this one helped gather up beetles as nimbly as could be. The palms of his hands flickered whitely as he worked, like the bellies of the May beetles. He threw them exclusively in Hermine's bucket. The next morning he greeted her with a laugh. Not a beetle would the Frenchman bestow on one of Hermine's pupils, although these were big girls by now, whom she should have been teaching how to cook, not how to gather May beetles. Outside of the glory, it's true, the beetles were of no use to her. As pretty as a single *Maikäfer* is, so are they disgusting in large numbers. They leak juice and stink and clump together. Her colleagues hated this assignment. They got sore throats, for already by the second cherry tree their feet were wet. Shoes were no good in those days. Hermine didn't dare tell anyone how much she liked it. It wasn't only the Frenchman, with his zeal against the German May beetles. It was also the early morning hour, the sparkling dew, the lovely countryside; it must have been the farmer's blood in her that made her so happy. But this came to an ugly end. The Frenchman waited until Hermine was collecting under the branch he sat on. Then he shook it. So one moment Hermine was the good girl in the story whom the tree showers with gold, and the next she was the bad sister covered with pitch. Like a monkey the dark young fellow landed next to her and began to pick the beetles from her hair and the back of her neck. Then he went looking for one that had, maybe, fallen down in front. Naturally that was going too far, and Hermine shrieked, as was proper. She sensed at once what was to blame: the whole week they hadn't been able to speak a single word to one another. Their sign language was too crude.

The girls, who hadn't liked the special favor of the May beetles, reported the incident. Then things went off like the Last

Judgment, especially since it was a racial offence. Only the fact that Hermine's brother was a leader in the Hitler Youth saved her from severe punishment. But she had to leave the lovely valley, again before the cherries were ripe.

Tomcat

This time Hermine thought: to my good luck! The next village lay high up on the Swabian Alb. The schoolhouse was new and its walls were made of almost nothing but windows. The purchase of curtains or shutters had been put off until better days. And so there was only the sun to disturb Hermine in her happy new competence. Though there was a tomcat. It was plain to see that the cat was in fact a tom, lying outside along the lower window sill, sunning himself and distracting the children. He was a magnificent, pitch-black tomcat, who belonged to somebody or other in the neighborhood.

During recess, the children wanted to pet him. But he wouldn't let them; he spat at them meanly. From Hermine alone he accepted a tender hand. Every day he rubbed himself against her legs and purred circles around her. Hermine was proud. Soon he was accompanying her up the staircase, for her room, there, was up in a tower. He sprang in front of her or ran along behind her. Then he sniffed over everything in her room. She offered him choice bits to eat, but for those hard times the tomcat was shamelessly finicky. Often she was sorry she had let him nose some delicacy instead of eating it up herself. One day, when she came out of the schoolhouse at noon, he was sitting in front of her door. That pleased her deeply. She opened up, and he made one mighty leap into the room and had his mouse. And from then on, he never sat before her door again. When she reached out to pet him, he bit, scratched and batted at Hermine, the same as anybody else.

Dog

From one day to the next, she was given notice that the inspector of schools would "pop in" to her first-period class, so he could "know" her as a teacher. "In what sense *know?*" she felt like saying; but it was no joking matter. Through the long afternoon until late in the night she prepared. She had the lesson down perfectly in her head—it could not go wrong. The sun, she knew, was still elsewhere in the world at such an early hour. The goodhearted school principal had warned her that this school inspector laid special value on teaching with visual aids. So she went very early—the tiny village was still silent, its streets empty—into the schoolhouse to arrange exactly the right visual aids just so on the nearly ground-level window sill. And as she did so, she saw that two dogs were outside, carrying on with one another. Actually there was only the one, big and shaggy, since the other, small and silky, all but disappeared under the coarse fellow.

The worst of it was that the big one simply wouldn't quit. Hermine banged on the window. He paid her no mind. Now she went out with the pointer to chase him away. He got angry, but she managed to save herself. She sat down with her back to the window to read everything through again, but to her irritation the dogs showed up on the other side of the glass schoolhouse.

Hermine stared fiercely down at her sketches or up at the blackboard, but the indecency was now in her eyes. Then came the sound of children, and, soon after, the inspector of schools.

Now, there is nothing more elusive than to give that perfect lesson. Hermine never learned how. Either she got lucky, or she didn't. When she succeeded, she felt that surge of concentrated power in her, in heart and mind. Then all was splendid between her and the children, an energy like balls flying back and forth and sparks soaring. After such a lesson she felt generous to all. The children beamed at her and crowded round. But the smallest trifle could let the power out of her again: a late child, an unfriendly colleague on the schoolhouse steps, the smallest slip in memory, any indisposition, a night without sleep. This time it was the cursed dog. Luckily the children of that time and place were still kind. They just gave no answers, or wrong ones. They whispered among themselves, rustled already with their sandwiches although it was only first period. After the lesson they glanced at Hermine with pity and made a wide circle around her.

She gave the same lesson the next day in another class. Now the sparks soared and the balls flew. Hermine yearned with all her heart for the absent school inspector. Afterwards the children hung from her arms and said, for her ears, the most intimate truths of their families. But unhappily the inspector of schools never heard any of that. He judged Hermine on the grounds of those sparks that hadn't flown. She was soon transferred once again. Not transferred as punishment, it wasn't so bad as that, but as a replacement for someone who was ill, to a place where, in those days, other, more dangerous sparks were flying.

Wolf

Things didn't go well for Hermine at this post. Various unfortunate factors came together. Mean principal, fresh children, apathetic colleagues, a bad inn in the town, a love affair gone wrong and, above it all, the air raids. She lived from holiday to holiday, for as bad as things were here, so were they good now at home. She liked it there so well that she kept the nights short, going late to bed and rising early, so that she could feel it for a longer time that she was at home. But all holidays came in due course to their dreaded end. In those days it took her a whole day to get back. In normal times the trip could have been managed in four to five hours. But now many trains were canceled; they were needed for more important transports. "No, I'm not leaving that early, by the first train. Somehow I'll get there eventually," Hermine thought, and took a later one.

And so that evening found her standing in the railway station in the city, three hours' walk from her workplace, and there was no other "somehow" but this to get her back there. Luckily my baggage isn't heavy, she thought, and bravely took up her middle-sized suitcase in one hand, her traveling bag in the other, and set off. She knew the way well. She had traveled this road plenty of times on her bicycle. It led down a valley that got narrower and narrower as it neared the town where her job was.

Although you were in a valley, you somehow felt higher up. The wooded slopes were darkening. But a half-moon shone in front of her. As far as the little hamlet that lay halfway there, the walk went fast and well. Only now and then Hermine had to switch her bags from hand to hand.

At the edge of the place she heard somebody's dog howling; at the other end of the hamlet was the dog itself, sitting untied in the road. He came up to Hermine, sniffed her, and it seemed to her that he looked at her trustingly. She had no great fear of him and walked on. But the dog followed. Mile upon mile she trudged; the dog was always there. Hermine's heart shrank inside of her. Once she had to stop and set down her bags for a while, and the dog growled at her. Now this was serious. True, he never came very close to her, just trotted along on the left side of the street. That she could still bear; it was only when he went on her right that she had a sense of being entirely powerless against him. Worst of all was when he ran at her heels. She broke out in a cold sweat. Then sometimes he ran in front for a time, and she could get her breath again. But then he sat down more than once and howled at the moon. He looked exactly like a wolf in the dark of the moonlit night. Gradually Hermine began to think this really was a wolf, who howled to alert his hunting companions on the wooded slopes that he had spotted prey. Every time she had to set her suitcase down she heard his growl. Attack me, then, leap for my throat, get it over with, she thought at last, but from then on she dared not put her baggage down again. Finally, in the distance, she saw the village. It was dark, blacked out on account of the air raids. The drone of airplanes, even enemy airplanes, would have sounded like salvation to Hermine by now; for the place was quiet as the grave. All the same she reached the first houses with a sense of huge relief. "Now I could scream and someone would hear me."

So she arrived at last at the garden-gate where she lived. When she opened it, to her terror the dog pushed close again with his muzzle. But once more it seemed to her that he looked up at her with trusting eyes, as at the start of their encounter. As she unlocked the house door, she looked back at him. The dog trotted away, but not in the direction from which they had come. Rather, he continued down the street and turned casually into an alleyway, as if it were something he did every day.

Now enlightenment struck Hermine like a blow. She dropped to the stair that led upwards to her room. The dog hadn't been from that other village at all, but rather from here, possibly from the very house next door. If she had just stroked him at once and spoken to him, they might have gone on without anxiety the whole way side by side, and each would have had a proper escort. Hermine sat on the staircase and wept.

The landlady came out of the door in her nightdress. "I'd have gone to the school in the morning and told them you weren't here yet," she said. Hermine was unable to speak. "But, miss, why ever do you look so? I'll let them know tomorrow that you're sick." Hermine pulled herself together, all the same, in what was left of the night, and was punctual to breakfast. The landlady was disappointed; she would have been only too glad for a reason to go to the school once again.

Ox

At the low point, Hermine finally had some luck. A school near home had a place for her. Mother took her back and set her soup bowl once again upon the family table. Hermine showed them her gratitude. On a summer day when she had the afternoon free and thunder and lightning threatened, she went out to the fields with them, to help with the harvest. They put a stick in her hand and let her drive the flies away from the oxen. The red-spotted one seemed to her the most troubled. She swatted, patted, slapped. When she turned her attention to the belly of the white ox, she got a butt from behind that sent her flying. When she came down again, she hadn't broken anything. Everyone laughed, for whatever the white ox did was always right. Probably he was insulted that Hermine had taken care of the red ox first, since he was the lead ox of the two. As it happened, he had been trained to pull with a horse, and he was rather famous in the place because he behaved like a horse himself. Under rein or shouted command, he handled amazingly well. People gaped to see them driving him at a trot to the mill, or even into town. He actually looked like a horse, a big white horse. His horns weren't thick and blunt like oxen's, but bent upwards slightly to delicate points. He had long since taught his red-spotted comrade the proper way to behave.

When it finally stormed, they picnicked. Afterwards they were still hungry, and the bread had run out. Hermine offered to fetch a fresh-made loaf from the bakehouse. This shed was some hundred yards from the farmhouse, on the edge of the orchard. And that was where the white ox now was grazing. He liked to graze once his work was done, and he grazed in just the civilized manner of a horse. They had to feed the red ox in the stall, since he romped around wildly and frightened people. When Hermine was halfway to the bakehouse, she heard a curious, angry noise and saw the lowered head. She ran for her life, but saw that she'd never get to the door in time to save herself. She pictured herself gored through and trampled. From behind her he came running like a wild beast, then stopped and stood still like a human, as if to let her pass. She stood in the doorway, and they gazed at each other. At first it seemed to her it was pity for her that she saw in the great dark-brown eyes. But then she saw that it was grief, a sadness bottomless and unfathomable. He turned away, back to his grass. Once Hermine had the loaf in hand, she walked right by him. She hadn't the slightest fear, and he never looked round at her. "Why are you so white in the face?" they asked, for usually Hermine's skin was rosy. "The white one came running . . ." They roared with laughter, and she couldn't explain.

The next summer the ox became more famous yet. He went mad. They had to haul him to the butcher prematurely, and in the middle of a workday. At first he grew testy with his red comrade: he wouldn't allow him to snatch so much as a bite of grass during their work; he even punched him with his horns. Then he got evil-tempered with his human co-workers. The sight of a woman's dress made him especially furious. Hermine's sister, who dealt with him all the time, had to put on men's trousers and hide her black hair under a hat, to everyone's amusement.

The white ox's grazing at the end of the day became dangerous, then out of the question. He obeyed no more commands without blows from a heavy stick. Hermine said she understood him: she had had a chance, once, to look him in the eye. She tried to explain that, from the grief she had seen there, rage was bound to come, rage beyond all reason, since there was no way out for him, as an ox, from his thwarted nature. They made cruel fun of Hermine for that. Mother said: "Naturally they're laughing at you. How can the ox even know, once he's grown, that they castrated him as a calf?"

Hen

The weeks of springtime in which the war came to an end and the victors marched in were strange: the farming folk were still afraid. But they had less fear now for life and limb. Instead they lived in dread that all order would be lost. For again and again, common soldiers came swarming over the property, to fetch calves and pigs out of the barns and to shoot into the chicken flocks. That caused fear. But soon officers came with them; sometimes there was even a German gentleman present, and what was most important: they had papers in their hands. They too took the best cattle, liveliest piglets and the rooster, all for nothing and again nothing. But they did it in an orderly way; thus it was rather a vexation than a cause of fear. The more decrees were issued, the calmer everyone felt. As spring came to an end, the tender hope was already budding that all might be put in order once again.

As a visible sign of this hope they had set the black-and-white-checked hen, as soon as she got broody as she did every ordinary spring, on thirteen eggs. At first they had a problem there: an egg trade had to take place with the neighbor, who still had his rooster. The brood-hen was ancient and especially large. They had kept her only for this purpose. Her old age she had thanks to her cleverness; she, along with six other hens, had escaped the French bullets. It was now nearly summer. Hermine and her mother were puttering around the kitchen one evening.

Suddenly a soldier stood before them. They started in fear, for they hadn't heard him coming. He was of a different race of men; perhaps he had that noiseless creeping up on his enemies in his blood. He roared: "Wine!" "*Nix* wine," Hermine said, instead of "We have no wine." Her mother fetched the jug of hard cider and offered the man a glass. He spat it out again. Then he pressed his rifle barrel in Mother's back and pushed her down into the cellar. Hermine went with them. One barrel had a cock in it. A sample of that stuff he spat out as well. The other barrels rang hollow. The soldier looked furiously around the cellar. But this was early summer in the cellar of a farmhouse. Except for empty cider barrels and a little heap of sprouted potatoes in one corner, there were only a few jars of preserves, moldy on top, on the rack. The black man was as unhappy as he could be when he made his way to the chickenhouse. This too was empty. Their few hens were already in the barn.

Just as the foreigner was about to go angrily away, the brood-hen came slipping out of the hole cut for chickens in the barn. Three weeks of sitting on the eggs had told on her: she was emaciated, and her feathers were dull and bristly. She clucked in excitement and ran in a great hurry to the chicken water. Anyone could see she was all in a fever, now, for the event close at hand. If a murderous thirst hadn't tormented her, she surely wouldn't have run away from the eggs before nightfall, to swallow greedily a couple of beakfuls of water. The French soldier raised his rifle. Hermine ran fast between him and the hen. "That's a broody-hen, you can't eat her," she cried. But he didn't lower the gun; Hermine looked down its black barrel. "Get away!" her mother shrieked. Then Hermine made a step to the side, the shot rang out, and the bullet whistled by her.

A few of them ran to the nearest neighbors, to see if they might have a brood-hen left. No one could help. To farmhouses any farther distant they weren't allowed to go so late in the evening; there was a decree to that effect. Whoever wasn't running around wailing for a brood-hen, was peering out the window. In the courtyard before the house, four more soldiers had made a fire and sat themselves down around it. Each of them was plucking a fowl. The evening wind blew the feathers over the whole farm. These fellows were adept at the plucking and gutting of animals. Then they sat a long time turning their spits at the flickering fire. It looked strange. In the meantime the moon had risen. A white sparkling came now and then from their dark faces, their teeth and eyes. They laughed rarely, never spoke especially loud, but their foreign tongue made the scene stranger yet. Hermine thought of the desert. Suddenly the men began to eat. The roasting had lasted a long while; gulping it down went quick. Hermine observed the one who was gnawing at the brood-hen. He ripped and bit at it with his strong teeth. Before long he threw his fowl away and reached for his neighbor's. There was a tussle. From another comrade he finally got a drumstick. All this happened quite fast. Just as hastily they put the fire out and went away.

The next day there was a lot to clean up. It looked sickening, the spot where the fire had been. Between sticks of wood and feathers lay tripe and bones, hens' legs and a pair of duck heads, besides the half-gnawed brood-hen. This rubbish went to the dung heap; on top of it came the thirteen eggs. When they were tossed on the pile, the shells broke. A few had already been pecked out from the inside. Probably they would have needed just the one night more. So many dead chicks looked ugly and desolate beyond all hope. That uncanny dread, the fear for order, overcame Hermine again. This time she even feared the chaos of darkest Africa.

Dog

On Hermine's way to school was a monastery with a chickenyard laid out along the front of it. Hermine was supposed to order a hundred chicks for the electric brooder. She couldn't find the chicken priest, so she went around to the feed kitchen, although it had a sign on it: "Beware of the Dog!" She was in a hurry, because school would start soon. A mean growl—she turned a little too slow to flee, and the bite on her leg brought her down to the ground. She rolled as far as the fence, just out of reach of the dog chain. It wasn't any chickenyard dog but rather a giant wolfhound that jumped against the chain again and again, getting wilder each time. She felt him hanging just above her. Once he sprang so violently against the chain that he rolled over himself. His scrambling legs humiliated him and made him even madder. Any moment the chain would break.

"I order a hundred chicks," she yelled at the chicken priest, who had been drawn by the hellish noise. He asked her over and over, "Who did you say wants them?" but all she could remember was, "They want exactly a hundred!" Hermine would know, after that, what it was to be in shock. It wasn't till the next day, in the hospital, that they got it out of her where she was born, and when.

The wound turned into an ugly scar. She had to leave to

others the practical fashion of the day, to go without stockings from early in the spring till late in the fall. All the children would have pointed at it and wanted to know what it was. From now on Hermine wasted many an hour darning stockings, but in fact she was lucky to have stockings: her younger brother paid for them with apples, and bacon.

Lamb

The textile shortage was general and great. A shepherd who passed through the neighborhood with his flock made a handsome profit from the situation. One of Hermine's sisters had to have a sheep at any price. For no small amount of food from their larder she had managed to turn up a spinning wheel and a loom. She wanted handspun, woven skirts that added curves. For a sack of flour, a lot of eggs and any number of slabs of bacon, she got herself a newborn lamb. It wasn't old enough yet to shear: it guzzled at its bottle and was soon the darling of the house. They hadn't known that lambs could jump so high. It sprang onto benches and tables. If Mother sat down, it jumped onto her lap and snuggled. It had learned that from watching Mother with the grandchildren. When it wasn't jumping or sleeping, it ran along behind somebody. It even ran after Hermine.

That spring they had a child going to first communion. For quite a while they'd been saving up sugar and trading potatoes for cocoa. It was going to be a lovely party. Hermine made a truly beautiful cake. On the eve of the holiday, after it had been sufficiently admired, she set it on the large table in the pantry. Another sister went to put her own precious offering beside it and screamed. The little lamb stood in the midst of the rubble that had once been a cake, licking buttercream from its belly. Hermine hadn't noticed that it was following her, and had let it in the pantry. The sister who had a healthy relationship with animals grabbed it by the scruff of its neck and locked it in the ducks' coop. There it bleated pitifully at first, then was silent. When they all thought—quite soon—the lamb had had punishment enough, they found it hanging by the neck between the high roof slats of the hutch. Next day the holiday mass invoked the name, more often than usual, of the Lamb of God, the innocent one. Not only the child awaiting communion but every member of the family wept copious tears. The most important son of the household was counted, at that time, among the missing. They cried for him long and often, but this day they cried for their lamb. Other people, as high-minded as they were mistaken, thought they saw through this weeping. They pitied Hermine most of all for her missing brother, since she cried the hardest. For a long time after, whenever she taught the schoolchildren the song about the little lamb that followed Mary, she had to fight back tears.

Horse

They still had a horse. But he was so old—over twenty years he had faithfully served them—that he was no longer fit for any work. Now he was only a gentle old soul. The brother who had been too young to be hauled off to war, and so had become the one in charge on the farm, couldn't bring himself to take Max to the horse-butcher. In the winter the horse ate the bread of charity in the barn. From spring until it was winter again, Max grazed half-blind around the vegetable garden. This went on maybe five years. Whoever came across him petted him and talked to him. Everyone liked him. The brother never forgot to bring him in at night.

In just those days when the French began marching in, Max fell sick. At the start of his illness he raged and thrashed about in his pain. It must have been a bad colic or a stoppage of the bowels. The mother knew that strong coffee from real beans would help, but they had none. She offered him the malt coffee, but he would no longer eat. After two days he gave up thrashing; now he only stamped with one forehoof hard against the ground. This he did always with the same foot and at regular intervals. It was terrible to have to see and hear this. Above all, the nights were bad; even in their bedrooms they heard the evenly measured clopping. They held their hands over their ears.

Hermine was tempted to pray for Max, that he might get better again or be able to die. For her the decline of the Fatherland was bound up with the image of the horse's slow dying; both were heavy and hard.

When they could no longer bear it with Max, Hermine set out with a younger sister for the veterinarian in the nearby town. They would have done this long ago, but it was forbidden to leave the villages. Only, the veterinarian's wife sent the girls about their business. "Because of an old, sick nag, when the world is going to ruin!" she sneered at them. Then on the way home it got dangerous. Suddenly they ran into a column of French soldiers marching. The chances for evasion were poor: on one side of the street was a steep bank, on the other a wide brook. They pushed their way through the bushes. A few soldiers took aim at them for fun with their rifles. One came out of the column. He pulled the smaller girl by the braids and pinched Hermine's breast. He would probably have done more. Then luckily another Frenchman presented himself. He struck the fresh one in the back with the butt of his rifle. He shouted at the girls. But no matter how loud he shouted, they still understood nothing. They wept and stammered about the veterinarian, the animal doctor. He must have been an educated gentleman; "doctor" he grasped. Probably he got the idea that their father was on his deathbed. So he gave orders again, to another man, to escort the girls. At first they thought they were going to be shot, but soon they perceived his kind purpose. They came across another column, marching with fiery red caps on their black heads. They would have been far more afraid of these.

When they came trembling home, Max was dead. For years they had had a Serb, a prisoner of war. When the war was won for him, he didn't come anymore. They thought he had gone away. But before he left the district, he came one last time, to show them that he had a revolver now. With this he shot his poor old friend, for he had loved him as the others did. The office of cadaver utilization was not yet functioning at that time. At the edge of the marshy meadow, by the three birches, they dug a hole, large if not deep. Here the grass grew greener and taller, a long while. Hermine often went there. She could see in the lush patch the shape of a horse.

Rat

Every evening they had a suitor at the house. He came from a rich family and was one of the first to return from the war unscathed. Just which one of them he was courting was not clear. A few, Hermine among them, had grounds for hope. She looked into the future and saw her troubles become as naught. One evening they all sat about as usual, waiting for the decision. Along came the sister who was no rival for the others—the one you could already have called the old maid—and said, I saw a rat. The hoped-for one took three candidates with him. Right away he locked all the kitchen doors and stopped up the cats' hole. "Pull everything away from the walls," he commanded. Only the stove and the granite sink stayed in their usual places. Then the girls were armed with broom, dustpan, potato-masher. He himself took up the poker. They all began to prod and pry.

Finally the rat was discovered. Hermine had imagined a far more terrible creature. She just looked like a frightened gray mouse. But she was quick! Whoosh, she was under the flour bin, under the kitchen cupboard, inside the slop bucket, then this was rolling together with its passenger across the kitchen, into the stove nook—cudgels flew. The man was in a frenzy. Someone rattled at the door, hoping to join the wild hunt. Hermine made to open it; he swore at her for that. Finally the rat was in a corner from which no escape was left for her. She tried all the same to climb the wall; the man beat her to death. Long after she was dead, he kept on beating her.

Then Hermine saw his face. Now, this was how she'd imagined a rat should look. His lips were pursed into a point. His nose was sharper than she'd noticed, his eyes bulged outwards and were hard and greedy. Afterwards he threw the bloody poker aside and sat himself down at the table to brag about his prowess at the hunt. Once the girls had cleared everything away, pushed the cupboards back where they belonged and wiped away the blood, he was still preening. It's true that by now he wore his normal face again, but Hermine saw the rat face on top of it and couldn't stop seeing it. And it was exactly the same for her sisters. Another girl entirely got a rich husband.

Riding Horse

Blutfreitag is a special day. It has no fixed date, and yet is so important that people are given to say: that was before Blood Friday, or that happened after Blood Friday. A holy object, a relic, a drop of Christ's blood mixed with earth, is taken out of the magnificent Basilica of Weingarten and carried through the city and the fields. All that is done on horseback, and countless riders from the whole region, horses and people in great numbers, pour into the small city. Only during the war was Blood Friday ever called off. But now that the war was over, riders' groups formed anew; many farmers bought a single horse, exclusively for that day.

Since time began, school has been out on Blood Friday. Hermine was using the day to sew clothes. Everyone, which is to say quite a crowd, was there, for it was raining so hard you could not step out the front door. In the days leading up to Blood Friday, the weather had been fine, but it had stormed in the night. Since then there'd been one cloudburst after another. Round about twelve someone said: "Looks like the procession's been canceled." For a horseman had just ridden into the village. Usually he wouldn't have gotten back home until evening. He was carrying the standard, and although the pennon should be stiff, they saw it drooping downwards in the distance, heavy with rain. It looked sad. Probably it made all of them think of their father. He had once been a zealous Rider of the Blood. For so-and-so many consecutive years of taking part, he had even gotten a medal.

One time he too had been allowed to carry the standard. He brought it home the night before, since at such an ungodly hour—Father had to set off at three in the morning—it couldn't be fetched out of the church. First Father bore the standard around house and barn. The children ran along behind him. Next he carried it ceremoniously through the orchard, a short way down the meadow and perhaps ten yards up the track into the fields. Afterwards it went through the stable, the cow barn and halfway into the pigsty. Father needed blessings wherever he could get them. The door to the chicken coop would have been too short even for the pennon. Finally the standard leaned in the front hall.

It was such a sanctified object that they hardly dared to whisper. That night their house seemed to them like a church. Since their father had been so honored, Mother took more children than usual with her to Weingarten. So Hermine had gone the one time to this event; she must have been about five. A crush of people, horses, more horses, finally the holy relic itself. All the people went down on their knees. Then horses again. "Here comes ours." Hermine's clever brother always saw things first. "God in Heaven, what a dreadful stomach-ache he must be having," Mother said, for their father's face was as grayish-white as the houses in Weingarten. He looked despairingly at his flock of children on the edge of the street.

Hermine hadn't liked it. The horses were always letting something drop; she felt it wasn't proper. Only the beautiful flight of stairs that led up to the church pleased her. Once you were on top it seemed that this was how heaven must be, with its booming organ. She never wanted to go again. All the same she looked forward to the day. Someone or other always brought back a little Holy Blood pendant, a copy of the relic that you could hang around your neck from a woolen thread and feel important, since it was so highly blessed.

But meanwhile the horseman had come nearer. It wasn't Hermine's younger brother: he wasn't the type to squander cash on a horse for such a purpose. He believed devoutly in the sanctity of money; he had traded their oxen promptly for a tractor. Everyone who was looking out the window saw that the rider was their neighbor; they saw how the water collected on the brim of his top hat and ran in a trickle down his neck. At the outset that had surely made him unhappy. But now that he hadn't a dry stitch left on his body, he appeared indifferent to it. The horse he rode looked equally wretched. Everything hung down from the animal: its tail, its head, its ears. Being soaking wet isn't right for horses, whether with sweat or with rain. Steeds must be fiery, and fiery surely means dry. The drenched nag now trudged by the window where Hermine was at her sewing-machine. She felt sorry for him; pity for him made her a little angry, so that she stopped attending to the finger that pushed fabric under the needle. The machine clattered irritably on and so did Hermine: "If that really was a drop of God's blood, He wouldn't be pouring down buckets today of all days—oh no!" The sewing-machine needle had just gone through Hermine's fingernail. Drawing the needle back up again hurt even more. "Well, there's a bit of striking evidence that it's God's blood after all," someone said. "Just punishment for blasphemy"—that from Mother. For many years after that, the fingernail had a furrow with a red spot in the middle—a drop of blood.

Goose

If the geese had been white geese, then this would never have happened. As it was, they lay, half grown, like gray stones in the farmyard in the early light. Hermine always had to be somewhere at some exact minute. She was in a hurry and ran over a goose with her bicycle. There was a great outcry, of humans and geese; she had no choice, however, but to go on her way. When she came home that evening, the poor goose sat in a warm nest in the stove nook with a splint on its leg and one wing bound to its body. Both were broken. They looked accusingly at Hermine, all the while stuffing cake into the goose's beak. The next day the creature was already limping around the kitchen. So the leg wasn't broken after all, but the wing was. When the bandage came off, it hung down pitifully. True, the goose could flap the wing up and down at regular intervals, but to hold it high was beyond her. The wing was sad but the goose flourished, got white and fat and terrorized the family dog.

    Hermine didn't like the pet goose. She said it was a proper humbug. As soon as the goose felt herself unobserved, she left off limping. And then she could hold up her wing quite a little while as well. "Because it was your fault, that's why you don't like her," they said to Hermine, and made a fuss over the goose. She might have rejoined the flock long ago, but now it was too late for that. She didn't dare leave the house anymore without a human escort. Even the rooster and hens attacked her. The neighbor's dog couldn't abide the sight of her. Only the cats slept next to her on the warm stove.

Before they went off to the potato field, they warned Hermine: "And look out for the goose!" Hermine had to sew clothes during the fall potato-holiday. She was concentrating hard at her clattering sewing-machine. When she heard the squawking, she thought: "Geese too—can't they just make a fuss over nothing!" But it got too loud: she looked out the door and was afraid. The flock of geese tugged and tore at something, pulled it this way and that like a white washrag. At Hermine's shriek the flock left off as if on command, ran away in lockstep and rose, all in a body, into the air above the tall apple tree. Hermine had never seen house geese fly so high. Their misdeed must have given them wings. She was afraid they would fly away altogether, *with shrill cry to the northland*, as the song went. A bit later, however, she saw the flock nervously grazing in the meadow.

Meanwhile Hermine had turned her attention to the victim. She smoothed the ruffled feathers and her tears fell into them. As she stroked it, the dead warmth of the goose moved her. She was entirely guilty for this sad fate. But then it was the still warm body that brought the loudest reproaches on Hermine. "If you had just chopped her head off while she was still like that, we could have roasted and eaten her!" For by the time they came home from the potato field, the goose was stiff and cold. From now on they couldn't abide Hermine about the place, where whatever she did ended in a muddle, and she was driven out once again. She looked for an apartment. But at that time they were even rarer than roast goose.

Rats

So Hermine was allowed to move in with the same uncle she had lived with once as a child, and who had never done her any wrong. Someone begrudged it to Hermine that she had found a new place to live. "That one's bad luck," this person told her old aunt, "see if you don't smell a rat ere long." When the aunt told the story, they all laughed heartily. Hermine hadn't been there long yet; they had played cards in the evening and were talking about this and that before going to bed. Then the dog pricked up its ears. They waited for a bark. But it didn't come; instead he tucked his tail under him and pressed himself, whining anxiously, against her uncle. At the house door they heard nothing, so the aunt went into the barn. That's what farm folk do, when something seems not quite right.

"Come quick," she cried. And they saw something extraordinary. The uncle's barn wasn't the most up-to-date: a long low trough with a rough wooden beam above it, that was the feeding apparatus. Now rats were jumping up to it from the floor: two rivers of rats flowed along the row of cows without slackening. Up front they sprang down to the floor again, came together without confusion in a single file and disappeared through the hole in the barn door that was there for the cats. Now, this endless flow of rats was so strange that humans and animals went rigid at the sight. The cows had gotten to their feet and hung back in their fetters, as far away from the rats as they could go. None of them moved. The cattle on the other side stood likewise frozen. The cat must have spat, at first; now she held still and showed her teeth. The dog stood motionless with his hair on end. Humans ventured neither word nor gesture. One heard only the scuttle of rat feet; it sounded as though water were running. And looked like water, as well. There must have been rats in the thousands. It seemed to them that an hour had passed before it was over.

No one had seen where they came from; no one saw where they went. Perhaps a rat catcher had lured them to their death in the water nearby. They ran as if under some relentless drive. The perfect order in which they went was uncanny. Human and animal alike sensed that they would turn vicious if this order was disturbed. A deep sadness came over Hermine. She felt sorry for her aunt and uncle. For the first time, she wished that she hadn't moved in with them.

Dog

As for the dog that had been so frightened of the rats: he and Hermine treated each other with great respect. By now she had been with her uncle for some time. One early evening when she came riding her bicycle home from school, the dog sat at the edge of the woods. This was still a goodly distance from the house. He showed his pleasure when he saw her and ran happily along in front of her the rest of the way. In time he was escorting her home from there every day. They told her, when she had had to be away all night, that he had come home inconsolable, would neither eat nor stir. The dog's behavior touched her. Without the slightest urging from her he had accepted her into his pack. Now she petted him in return.

During the summer holiday she went away for a couple of weeks, and when she came back again, the dog was almost beside himself with joy. He jumped high in the air, bit his own tail, barked out his jubilation. And even days later he would remember and fall again into transports of joy. Now Hermine caught herself thinking of the dog while she was at work. And when she did, a gratified feeling, even a mood of elation would come over her. Then hastily she shook her head and turned red. "As if I were in love," she thought. When she pedaled homewards, she looked forward almost indecently to seeing him, sitting and waiting for her by the wayside. Soon, when she went to school, the dog began to accompany her, first as far as the woods, then all the way through them.

One day he wanted to go even farther with her. She scolded him: You can't come to school with me, now go home. In cocky excitement he ran along the street beside her. Thus they came to a farm where there was a mean dog on a chain. The bad dog shot out of his doghouse, fastened his jaws on the neck of Hermine's friend and shook him to death.

Hermine was ashamed of the ridiculous sorrow that refused, now, to let her go. She even had the urge to dress all in black on account of it. Of course she didn't do it, but all the same her deep mourning for the dog colored her life for a long time. "Because of an animal," her old aunt sneered at her. "Because of a dog," her uncle growled, and she sank a bit in his esteem.

Animals on the Road

Because she had a long way to go, Hermine needed a vehicle. When times got better, the vehicle got a motor. First, a motorbike. Almost as soon as she had it, however, and was driving it cheerfully homewards through the night, she ran into an animal. When she managed to free her wounded foot and set the motorbike back in gear again, she was bowled over again by this creature, which came running at her from the other side. Now she saw that it was a badger. She knew these animals only from their pictures. Another time she had a crash on account of a young wild boar; yet another, a demented dog knocked her over.

Her uncle had a sick cow. How is she doing, Hermine asked at breakfast. "Going bit by bit," he said sadly. That night when Hermine rode her expensive conveyance onto the threshing-floor that doubled as a garage, the dead cow was lying there, and she drove over her stiff leg. It gave her such a violent fright that she forgot to fasten gate and lock alike.

That night the bike was stolen; next, Hermine bought an auto, a used Volkswagen Beetle. Now this vehicle she recognized from the first as a weapon against every creeping or flying thing. But it also allowed her to get acquainted with her future husband. For a time, she was in heaven when she drove. The streets were wider there, and one could go fast and yet think about other things. Suddenly a hedgehog embarked upon one side of the street, hoping to reach the other. He managed to complete this itinerary; Hermine, meanwhile, hardly had time to brake; the car behind her, no time at all. He laid a paper on the roof of his car; Hermine allowed that she alone was the guilty party, and signed it. It was the kind of debt which this world rarely forgives. She paid for a long time.

Wife

Tick

One fine Sunday Hermine went driving with her fiancé along the lake. At last they found the right spot. In a dense clump of bushes Hermine pulled her bathing suit on. She was thinking of going straight into the water, but he was, even back then, a man who planned ahead. Then you'd have to sit there the whole time in your wet things, he pointed out. And besides, they had a lot to talk about.

For that morning their coming marriage had been announced from the pulpit for the first time; though only for Hermine's kith and kin, in her home village, in her church. They were discussing what guests should be invited to the wedding, and this brought them to the food that would be served. And that in turn landed them on the subject of money. "First that car has to be paid for, before we get into anything too fancy," the fiancé said. Just then something itched on Hermine's left breast. He was for the combining of their incomes, he went on, and for the management of them by one person, namely himself. Now it itched Hermine so much that she really had to scratch it, but she couldn't get at it, since in those days bathing suits still had "bones," not their own bones, of course, but whalebone stays. "Your finances are in miserable shape"—that was it, Hermine couldn't stand another moment. She ran back into the bushes, to see what was itching her.

Then she was alarmed. Near her nipple she had a second one, likewise small and dark brown. She tried to pull out the tick, but it wouldn't let go. It came back to her that these creatures sooner leave their heads behind than give up their hold, and that causes a serious infection. She didn't want an infection in that place, not for her wedding night. Feeling completely out of sorts, she came back. And now he said he wanted to love her a little. But that was exactly what she couldn't bear the thought of. "What's wrong with you, all of a sudden?" he asked. "Headache," she said, although the pain was hardly in her head. While she was dressing herself, she understood that the tick too had made herself a new home—a house like a farmhouse, with a round, hot, dark red barnyard around it.

Piglet

After a lot of going back and forth it was decided: At least the civil ceremony would take place in Hermine's home village. For she was proud that in spite of everything she had gotten herself a proper husband. She wanted to show him off at the town hall, in front of all the people. And she wanted to cut a figure as she did so. So there was a lot more going back and forth about what she should wear. In the end she decided on a black suit, especially since her old aunt had said that no married woman could manage without one. Therefore Hermine bought an expensive one, even though she badly needed the money for other things.

The registry was open on Saturday morning in the same hours when children were supposed to be in school. Hermine had to teach that class early, and it seemed to her that Friday afternoon would never end. Shortly before it finally did end, Hermine was called to the telephone. As she hurried down the long hall—she was teaching by now in a small nearby city—she was afraid of only one thing: that her fiancé had changed his mind and was backing out at the last moment. But it was something else. A farmer from her village, the vice mayor, was at the other end of the line. He complained that the regular mayor, the next day, had urgent business in Tübingen, so now he would have to perform the wedding himself. "What else is a vice mayor supposed to do?" Hermine thought. But he yammered on: "I absolutely have to be at the pig market tomorrow. These piglets are plenty big, I can't feed them another week longer. Come tonight with your witnesses, but not too late or the town hall will be closed." He hung up.

Hermine drove in a hurry into her future city, to pick up her fiancé. She stood in a shabby summer dress at the gates of the factory. She was only wearing this dress at all because she had washed and ironed all her decent clothes in preparation for her marriage. She had thought to leave this one threadbare frock behind her, in case she should ever want to help with the haying. Finally he came out: a man who didn't give up his own old stuff without a fight. He even had knickerbockers on, of a kind that nobody else had let himself be seen in for a long time. He laughed out loud. The first marriage witness was still at the building site, but once he took off his dirty white coverall, he looked more or less presentable. The other marriage witness had been baking and cleaning all day, since the reception after the ceremony the next day was to have been at her house. She insisted on pulling on stockings, at least.

At the town hall the cleaning woman was banging away. The vice mayor hadn't yet shown up. When they went by his farmyard to make perfectly clear they were ready, they heard a great fuss coming from the pigsty. "Just two more," the farmer yelled above the piglet that he was making handsome for its sale the next day. He had a black-and-white breed of pigs. The little pig that he grasped by its hind leg and that screamed so piteously had white ears. The last piglet was entirely black; this one liked being scrubbed. He held still and grunted his satisfaction. Then he was visibly disappointed when the farmer cut it short. Hermine whispered her apologies—it was just that she had to be at the registry right away.

The regular mayor had left all the papers ready in the best room of the town hall. His deputy held the papers far out in front of him. He needed glasses badly, but nothing gets in a farmer's way more than a pair of glasses. So he read haltingly, who they all were and to what end they were gathered there. The marriage witnesses could have testified to all that, and would have been glad to add that he stank emphatically of the pigsty.

The black suit hung for years with Hermine's summer clothes, then with her winter clothes, then with the summer again, by turns. Somehow every time she looked at it, a sleek black piglet came to mind. When she finally had occasion to wear the thing, it was too tight, and entirely out of fashion besides. Fully unworn it went into the bag of used clothes.

Pets

They had a child. Hermine wanted to teach her to be kind to animals. Together they fed the swans along the shore. Once the child refused to leave them. Hermine had to be somewhere; she insisted that the child come away. She was about to turn and praise her obedience, for the little girl, she thought, held tightly to her skirt. Then something pinched her fiercely in the calf. It was the swan, who had pursued her up the stairs. The little one came running happily after, because Mama was taking the swan home with her. Not at all; he was biting Mama, Hermine said. The child was pleased: "He's mad, because you won't let me stay here." It did look that way.

They were on a walk around a large pond. A robin redbreast sat on the path and let itself be caught without a struggle. Papa and the child carried it by turns in their cupped hands. He would get a cage for it, he said. Hermine saw herself catching flies and digging worms. The path around the pond took an hour to walk; the cupped hands began to ache. Now Hermine took a turn. Hardly was the little bird in her hands when it was well again, beat about like a wild thing until she had to let it fly away.

Now a bird was on their minds and a cage had been promised. They bought a parakeet. Father and daughter were in a great hurry to teach him to speak. After a few days they turned the task over to Hermine. But as soon as she gave her attention to the bird, its feathers began to fall out. Before long she saw that the bird could no longer grasp its perch. It sat sadly on the floor of its cage. Hermine soaked a cotton ball in ether. Long after, she could feel in her hands the small hard thumping of the bird's heart as it died.

June felt like winter, and the child found a swallow that looked dead in the street. In a nest of wood shavings by the stove, to Papa's amazement, the bird came back to life. When Hermine came home, they wanted her, too, to admire the little swallow. But hardly had the bird felt Hermine's eyes upon it when it flew full force out of the nest and into the windowpane. Hermine tried to open a window but its panic only mounted; three, four times it flew against the glass, and then it was really dead.

The cage was empty yet again. They bought a golden hamster. Then like every family with a hamster they bought another hamster and another, for one way or another these little animals easily depart their cages or this world. They had a Susi for quite a long time. Unfortunately, she sat on Hermine's chair; Hermine did likewise. Crying, the child called Papa on the telephone; together they thought up a name or two for Mama that pointed rudely to her country origins.

Soon after that, as luck had it, the little girl found a hedgehog. She called him Hannibal and carried him around with her wherever she went. A hedgehog will even let you pet it. While the child was still asleep, Hermine saw Hannibal lying on his back in the garden, paddling his feet weakly in the air. She hurried out to right him again, found instead a gruesome wound in his belly in which maggots already swarmed. Full of horror, she buried him in a pile of leaves in a nearby park. Then she washed all the clothes the child had worn in the days of the hedgehog. The little girl looked around the garden for her friend for a long time.

After that, turtles came into fashion. Fathers drilled holes in their shells and tied them out in the yard like dogs. They dragged themselves to the ends of their ropes and scratched and dug till they buried themselves. A woman next door was mowing the lawn, saw her daughter's turtle too late and mowed off its leg. Hermine had to watch out for that! Next time she took out the lawnmower, her heart nearly stopped. Where the turtle's head should have been was a red lump. Trembling, Hermine bent for a closer look: the creature was merely busying itself with an overripe strawberry. All the same Hermine cut the rope. "No one can have an animal with you around," her husband said. The child looked at her resentfully.

Wild Boar

"You two need to get out into nature. Look around at the animals." That was Hermine talking. Every weekend she wanted to get out of the city, to wander through woods and fields. The child liked to go; her husband often had to be begged. At a fork in the path, they had a difference of opinion. He said right, she said left and was pigheaded about it, and they went left. It turned out to be the wrong trail, narrowed, then disappeared altogether. They had to jump over ditches and crawl under barbed wire. "We always have to do it your way! This is absolutely the last time that I'm going along with it." That was how the conversation went for a long time. The argument was embarrassing to the child. She kept her distance.

Now, here at last was the hiking trail, well known to both of them, the one named after the famous naturalist. That was it, Hermine's husband hadn't another word to say to her, only marched away at a fast pace. But they had quite a long way to go yet, through a dense pine forest at that. They were half-grown fir trees; on both sides of the path they grew so thickly that their lower branches were scraggly. You couldn't see a yard into the woods. The twilight sky made a narrow stripe above the path. It was so quiet it was eerie. The child came running up and took Hermine's hand. Then something crackled nearby in the young pine forest, or rather it was a noise like something breaking. "It must be a big animal," Hermine thought. There came another sound she had heard one time as a child, when one of their pigs went wild. "What is it?" the child whispered. Hermine said, even more softly, that she didn't know. At the same time she had read not long ago that wild boars lived in the thick woods hereabouts. She knew, as well, that the males of the species could be dangerous, especially if they were irritated. Probably this one took their walking through his woods as an irritation—for the ugly, angry grunting had turned more menacing.

Hermine had never lived through a fear like that before. She imagined sharp tusks and slit bellies; her knees trembled, her hands grew cold and wet and sweat stood out on her forehead. "Papa," the child whispered again and again. If the fear of death hadn't stopped Hermine's throat, she might have taken the opportunity to enlighten her young daughter: She should never put her faith in a man, there was no relying on them, etc. For the nearer the grunting sounded, the angrier she was at her husband. He walked with a stick; he was obligated to protect her and even more so their child. She made up her mind that if she came out of this alive, she would never speak to her husband again. Suddenly the woods came to an end. It wasn't quite dark.

And there stood Papa, leaning on his stick. The child ran to him. Hermine looked around her uneasily. Nothing was hunting her. Her husband had taken the tired child onto his shoulder. From up there she looked down on Hermine a bit scornfully, or so it seemed. He wouldn't look at her at all; that appeared to be the plan he had hit upon. Only once she was driving them home and didn't know how to turn the lights on did he look at her again. Then he showed her what to do.

Snake

The child was already in school. She still liked to walk and so they went hiking one Saturday afternoon along the Argen. "There's a blindworm up there on the path," said Hermine. The child wanted a look at the supposed blindworm. Hermine had forgotten how fast she could move. She heard the cry. As soon as the child's shadow fell across the snake, it raised its head and bit her in the hand. Then it disappeared in the grass, but first Hermine saw the unmistakable cross on the back of the viper. She sucked at the wound, which was no more than four fine needlepoints. Neither blood nor poison came out of them. Cutting would be necessary; but even if she had had a knife, she couldn't have brought herself to cut the child's hand. So they bound the arm up tight and ran.

In the hospital no one was in a hurry; it was still a Saturday afternoon. Although Hermine whispered snakebite, and viper, plainly enough, the nurse took in a knife-wound first. Then all at once they tore child from mother with a violence that belied the long wait in the waiting room. Hermine was summoned, much later, by the doctor in charge. He had been on holiday, he said, had come in especially for this case. In his day he had seen, and treated, about everything that could happen to the human body, but never a snakebite. Nevertheless he had done what he could: telephoned the institute in the tropics, had antivenin delivered from some distant depository, cut and injected. The child was not yet out of danger. Hermine told the doctor: I sent her to look at it. He gazed at her without understanding. Then what a night she passed!

The next day it was clear that all would be well. The doctor was pleased: now he had seen it all, and returned to his vacation. The child, in time, learned to hide the peculiar scars with her other hand. But when anyone asked Hermine how the girl had gotten those marks, she would say with pride: "A snake bit her."

Bull

Now the girl had lots of friends, and lots of homework as well. She didn't want to hike with her parents every weekend anymore. One fine fall day Hermine talked her daughter into it. For three full hours they walked. Hermine was downright proud of the magnificent countryside. It was almost as if she had painted the colorful woods herself. And she felt, beyond that, an elation she had seldom felt: for the intact, harmonious family, enjoying nature together as one.

Towards evening they started up a hill. A farmer was driving a great herd of cattle down it, towards his barnyard. He came to them and said they should stay where they were, there was a bull in the herd that didn't like strangers. So which hunched back belonged to the unfriendly bull? They had plenty of time to pick him out, but still they couldn't tell. The herd loitered and idled along. They had all had enough to eat; no cow was eager for the barn. For their part the three wanderers were getting hungry, and hunger urged them on. Only two last cows dawdled outside the barn door, near where they were waiting. Then Hermine heard the sound that was too well known to her, an angry sound between a snuffle and a bellow. She saw the lowered head. Her girl and her man were not so quick to grasp what was happening. Ready to die, she put herself in front of them. The farmer, however, had also understood the language of the bull. He was still able to cut off his charge, and to beat his ringed nose bloody.

Dog

Hermine exercised a strange power of attraction over all stray dogs. Big shaggy fellows and dainty poodles alike made bigger and smaller circles around her, when they were all out walking. Hermine wondered more than once if the Devil was at work. Most of these, it's true, were bone-headed young mutts that just wanted to give her their paw or fetch sticks. Some sat quietly waiting beside her bench until she walked on. It happened again and again that one tried to get into the car with her. Hermine had it hard to fend them off, although with one angry glance and a masterful shout her husband could send them packing.

Once, at eleven, Hermine was about to start boiling potatoes, when she glanced at the kitchen calendar. No potatoes today—it was her anniversary. She ran quick to the butcher. "Two well-aged steaks, please, one large, one small." The price shocked her. Then there was a dog behind her, a scary one. She crossed to the other side of the street. He followed her. She turned into an alleyway. He was waiting for her. He stayed hard at her heels; the faster she went, the closer he stuck. She was on the point of offering up her little steak. Surely he would have gulped it down in one mouthful and demanded her husband's big steak as well. When she got close to home, Hermine started to run. She was up the steps in one stride, but when she turned the key, there he was. She pressed herself through the doorway—muzzle and paw were between the door and the jamb. She was winning the fight with the muzzle: she beat it violently with her pocketbook. But the dog kept his foot in, stubbornly, as pushy as a door-to-door salesman. It was a wild scramble there on the doorstep. She really had to hurt the dog, to stamp hard on his paw, before he gave up a howl and she slammed the door shut.

All that had upset Hermine. Meat cookery requires the fullest attention, if a chop is to be tender and done just right. She said to herself, now I won't have enough time. But then she had plenty of time, more than she needed, so that the steaks were tough as leather. The flavor was off as well. Her husband ate his sullenly. "Out buying meat on a regular weekday," he grumbled. She murmured something about a sale. They chewed hard and in silence; that this was a special day, a day to celebrate, never entered his mind. Hermine couldn't talk about the dog. Earlier, years earlier, she had tried to tell that kind of story, to explain that kind of experience to other people and herself. In the best cases she had reaped incomprehension for her trouble, more usually disapproval, ridicule most often of all. Inside of her she had a secret chamber for such things. What had happened to her today was already within, and the door shut tight.

Bees

Now came bad times. Hermine's husband got sick. Many months went by, and her only encounters, as she drifted from bench to bench, were with pigeons and sparrows. Sadly Hermine read the walkers' tips and trail reports in the newspaper. Another teacher at the school, the greatest hiker of all, wrote these columns, splendid in both words and pictures. In the past Hermine had eagerly gone wherever they sent her. One proposed walk attracted her particularly.

On a Sunday she talked her husband into it. That place wasn't hilly, she said; by now he could surely manage it. When he still wouldn't go along with her, she pointed out that movement was good for his health. The hike started out well. The little village was pretty, the slope shady, the path smooth. According to the trail report they should strike out across open field, towards a little woods in which there were benches to rest on. But they also saw the bank of storm clouds gathering behind the woods. After perhaps a hundred yards, her husband began to complain: he was hot, it was hard going, his chest felt tight. By now the sun was scorching, although it had been overcast when they left. Should they go back? "Not uphill," he almost shouted. Hermine felt fear, and the prick of a bad conscience. They found a shortcut, a wagon track across the field, and then they saw ditches that they could walk along. There were boxes on the side of the ditch.

When they drew near, they heard what these boxes were for. With a storm coming on, the bees were in a bad temper. They buzzed poisonously. Just go by in a hurry—they went by, and as they did, the bees, all of them, attacked Hermine's head. She had a fresh permanent; that was what upset them. Her husband said: "It serves you right." But it was horrible, this hot, angry buzzing in her hair. Then they found the bottom of her hair: stings behind her ear, on the back of her neck, on her forehead. Hermine began to scream. Now her husband took pity on her. He took off his shirt. He wound her head in it like a mummy and beat at it with his hands. It hurt, but the buzzing came to an end. All this while they were running away. Her husband picked the dead bees out of her hair. He counted them as he searched, and announced the total: twelve. The arithmetic irritated Hermine. When they were walking again, she asked him how big her head was. "Same as usual." She had been thinking it was gigantic. After that she had no more questions, for she had begun to feel sick to her stomach. Now he asked her again and again how she was doing. She couldn't answer. She only wanted to reach the woods, so she would be spared dying under the hot sun.

The hiking expert hadn't promised too much. There were the benches, and water beside them. Her husband dipped up handfuls of it onto Hermine's head. It did her good. Under her wet hair he found the stingers. Meanwhile the storm arrived. A cooling wind blew all around Hermine's wet head. Arm in arm they walked to the little village through the driving rain.

Stag

Hermine liked one of the other teachers. During recess she sat next to him at the big table. They had things in common. They didn't much care for the same cheeky pupils, had the same complaints about the rector and thought the same woman the nicest of their colleagues. He always had something to talk about, especially on Mondays. As it turned out, he was a hiker too, only he hiked in the mountains. He told her all about it and described the most glorious rambles. Hermine could only dream of such pleasures. Usually he walked by himself; but time after time he invited Hermine to walk with him. The thing was of course impossible. But all at once one day it was possible. Her husband was traveling on business, her daughter was in England with her school class.

Very early of a Sunday morning he came to get her. And then they went hiking. He had picked out a fine, long loop for them. The views were magnificent, and all day long they gazed, were uplifted, rhapsodized. He knew the name of every peak and she of almost every plant. And so they never ran out of things to talk about. Towards evening he stopped and said: "We're still an hour away. But we could cut across the mountain and make it to Dornbirn in time to eat." Hermine was for eating in Dornbirn.

The climb was steeper than it looked. She let her light-footed colleague go first while she clambered after him, panting and red in the face. "Here's the crowning moment of the day," her escort called down to her. And he pointed at a giant stag that stood on the trail to the summit. But as they continued up the path, the stag didn't flee, as is proper for a stag; instead it came towards them. They were frightened. Her colleague went pale, and ran back down the mountainside like a scared rabbit. Hermine wasn't about to go that way again; she stayed where she was. Meanwhile the stag fell into a peculiar trot. She could already see his light-brown, stupid eyes. She didn't know how these animals went about it: whether they gored you, impaled you or trampled you to death. However it happened, her false step would come to light. For in the face of the stag's antlers it became quite clear to her that her action on this fine day had been a false step. Suddenly reason came back to her: a horned animal that is about to attack sinks his head, while this one held his rack of antlers high and proud. "He's tame," she cried down into the chasm. Now the stag was there, and allowed her to pet him. Her colleague came nearer, timidly, and the stag looked down at him. Man and stag couldn't stay long that way, eye to eye. When the two people began to walk again, the animal followed close behind. The antlers so close at their backs made them uneasy. They tried to get the stag to take the lead, but he simply stood where he was. So with the horns behind them they came over the mountain. Finally they left him behind.

"That was quite a thing," was all her companion had to say; otherwise he spoke no more. Likewise when they drove through Dornbirn, not another word about stopping somewhere to eat. The line at the border crossing was very long, and while they waited the speechlessness grew into a physical thing, jerky, awkward, and all the more embarrassing. When Hermine at last got out of the car, she could barely thank him for the lovely day she'd had, for sheer exhaustion, or sorrow. The silly stag had not only ruined the day, from evening on; he had wrecked the friendship. On Monday, during recess, her colleague still had nothing to say to her. This time, of course, she knew it all already. But the following day he sat himself down with that woman teacher who, they both used to say, was the nicest of all the others.

From now on it was a trial instead of a pleasure to sit at the big table. Hermine bent one ear to her neighbor while the other ear strained jealously to pick up every word from across the wide tabletop. So Hermine lost all interest. More and more often she sat at her desk all through recess and was startled when the children, in no time at all, came trooping noisily in.

Cat

Heavily laden, Hermine dragged herself down a long hall to the last schoolroom. She was carrying a display frame along with its stand, the box of scissors, the bag of fabric scraps and the yarn sack; her own briefcase was clamped under her arm. Some version of this was the way she always traveled these days. It was the time of the classroom shortage; therefore some classes migrated from room to room and she had no choice but to follow; and almost all the rooms were emergency classrooms of some sort. It was furthermore the time of the great overcrowding, when new pupils were coming in waves. Hermine taught hundreds of children a week. And on top of that it was the time of the teacher shortage. To fill out its curriculum the school had had to perform the most grisly contortions.

Hermine was now on her way to fifth and sixth hour, the last two hours of school. The children still had enough left at the end of the day for the subject she taught. So why did no child come to her aid? Just before the doorway her briefcase came sliding down. She leaned it up against the wall with her foot, meaning to fetch it presently. With her free elbow she pushed open the door. And then she saw why no child had come to help. There was a cat in the schoolroom. No doubt they had all fooled around a good deal with cats, but inside the school it was something different. Every child wanted to hold it. Hermine let them be: maybe one was a child who, after all, had never held a cat in its arms. Finally the cat had had enough. They let her out through the window; it was a sort of cellar window. Hermine shouted, now, that they really must begin: today they were going to learn something new. Children can always be enticed by something new. When the bell rang for sixth period, nobody asked to go to the bathroom. But when the bell rang school's-out, they rushed for the door.

Hermine set off on the return trip with her burdens and there was her briefcase: it was still leaning against the wall. Somehow it had about it a slight look of insult and dishevelment. She took out her keys, in order to lock up the school and open her car door—and saw that her purse was missing. It was no ordinary change purse that had disappeared, but rather a large, handsome leather wallet; her husband had given it to her especially because she was occupied with money so much more than she wished. She was constantly buying material for all those children. In the stores she haggled down to the last percent, added up, rounded off, and even so it seemed to her she was always laying out too much. Most of the time she didn't care to run up a debt in a store and so dipped into her own household money. The summer vacation was the only time her accounts came out even.

Collecting the money was disagreeable in itself. True, a fraction of the children brought it promptly and reckoned to the penny. Hermine knew in advance which ones. Others forgot about it week for week. Some came crying and said they had lost it, or part of it, and Mama wouldn't give them any more. And others again insisted they had already paid. Her wits sharpened by experience, Hermine pointed out that there was no record of this. But at once witnesses were produced who had seen with their own eyes that their friend really did pay. Some threw the money at Hermine, after a long recital of begging and coaxing, with looks on their faces that said, "There, if you're absolutely determined to get rich at my expense." Again and again a child gave back to Hermine the sturdy wool or piece of fine linen, so carefully cut out, and tried to use in its place some flowered rag or flimsy synthetic thread. And that made trouble for both of them, Hermine no less than the child. To avoid which, she went to such pains to organize the money. It had gone on, in fact, that morning: she had bought beads and string for the third grade. She was teaching 3A, 3B and 3D, about forty students a class—one mark, fifty-five *pfennig* per child. The children liked the wooden beads of many colors and made haste to bring the money, all except a couple of incorrigibles who forgot. At recess some even came running from 3C, the first class she taught the next day. Hermine would have sooner had peace, just then, than payments. All the same she was full of praise for the children.

To look for the thief was useless. The toilets were at the end of that long hall. In two hours' time a lot of children passed that way alone, including the bigger ones. Once before, and not all that long before, the same thing had happened to Hermine. That time, true, the money had been less, and the briefcase had been in the schoolroom. When she reported the theft to the office, they had made fun of her: it was her own fault. She expected no better this time. Hermine wept with rage. Then there was the cat, strutting across the schoolyard with its tail held high. The whole kitty, out the window, she thought to herself—and she laughed, again with rage.

Raven

One third grade had her for an art teacher. With children so young, art worked best as part of the regular class, Hermine thought. But this was the time of specialization, and so an art teacher was suddenly prized. Maybe Hermine hadn't slept so well; one day she thought up the theme: "Let's draw a black animal." Who would have thought there were so many black animals? In no time the children had come up with a whole list: stallion, dragon, raven, blackbird, cat, bat. They got out their black crayons. All of their black crayons were still long, since they hardly ever used black. Right from the beginning, the lesson went wrong. They began to draw the whole list of black things as a row of tiny figures on the paper. "No, you should pick out just one animal to draw, and draw it big," Hermine instructed.

Then when she walked among their desks, she saw how one boy—who was known to be a bit difficult—had begun to fill up his drawing paper with black from bottom to top. "The background of the animal has to be light. A stallion could be standing in a green meadow, the black cat might be lying on a colored tablecloth, the blackbird could be sitting in the middle of flowers." But when she came back to that little boy, already a quarter of his sheet was black. So she said to him kindly: "Now you have a nice black floor. You can put a spotted cat on it." He looked hostilely at Hermine. Next time she came to look, his sheet was two-thirds black, and the black was as dense as could be.

Hermine tried again: "That's a field of black dirt. Now draw some colored flowers on it." Wildly, the little boy began to smear the last bit of white space with black. She was about to correct him when he kicked her in the shin with his big shoe. He even struck at her face with his fists. He knocked her glasses off; luckily they didn't break. Then the boy buried his face between his crayon-blackened fingers, and stayed that way for the rest of the class. Hermine let him be. When she saw the tears leaking through his black fingers, she felt sorry for him: He could draw a red car or whatever he wanted—but he didn't want to.

At the end of the hour, she collected the sheets. The results were sad. Only one talented artist had managed to draw a handsome raven on a branch, and two nice little girls had placed black cats on tablecloths. All the rest were ugly monstrosities of virtually indeterminate species. She had to tell one little boy: "The Devil isn't an animal." Ever after, when she taught that art class, she stuck with trees and flowers, suns, houses and people.

Owl

That night, Hermine first slept for an hour, then woke up and heard the owl cry. She was queerly hot and running with sweat. At once she thought of the child she had plagued with correction until he fought back. The more she reflected on it, the plainer it was to her that she had been in the wrong. She couldn't get back to sleep for thinking about it. She would make it up to him the next day. But the next day there was no making it up to him, and Hermine waited for the owl's cry. Only at the first glimmer of dawn it came. Although she'd been waiting for it, it made her afraid; she trembled, and the strange heat came over her once again.

It was the first of the nights when Hermine did not sleep—just so suddenly it began. Sometimes the owl awakened her after that first brief sleep, sometimes at midnight. Many times she waited for the owl until it cried at dawn; at other times it didn't cry at all. She was caught in a devil's knot by the cry of an owl: when it didn't cry, she lay awake and listened for it; when it did cry, she couldn't sleep for dread. And then, on account of that shrieking in the night, she could no longer abide much shrieking during the day. "She's getting red in the face again," the children whispered, and they laughed. Those perfect lessons, high times of elation for heart and mind, hardly ever happened anymore:

nights of the owl consumed them, in hindsight as in prospect. It was a misfortune that this should be exactly the time when everything old was out. Up until now Hermine had been able to take a certain pleasure, daily, weekly, yearly, in simply fulfilling the requirements. Now she couldn't even understand, from the instructions, exactly what was required. Her second-graders and fourth-graders were shrieking louder from month to month, probably because they, likewise, didn't know anymore what was required.

Hermine tried to cover her failure with exaggerated diligence. A strange zeal for order overtook her. All night long she sat there, trying to make her pupils' aprons and potholders all nicely finished and alike. "What kind of new craziness is this?" her daughter wanted to know. When the owl cried for the first time, winter had been on the way out. Hermine thought, "She's looking for a mate." But the owl was still crying when spring came to an end. "Maybe she's having a second brood." And when winter began again, she listened for the owl to cry, first out of hunger, and then again in search of her mate. Hermine began, naturally enough, to cry out too. She complained. She soon noticed, though, that nothing is more boring to other people than somebody else's sleeplessness. There were some among her relatives who simply didn't believe her. Her doctor had said it himself: People tell you they haven't slept a wink all night, when actually they've lain awake for barely an hour. So she quieted down about it, especially since, with her rosy cheeks, no one could see it in her.

Sometimes she played with the idea of painting black rings around her eyes, like those the young girls were wearing, so that people would see what she suffered. And on top of that, no one but she ever heard the owl. She asked all the women who lived nearby. One time she even stopped a stranger on the street. She only knew that the woman lived in the neighborhood, and that she herself looked worn out, as though she hardly slept. Hermine asked whether she heard the owl in the night. Did she come from the asylum in Liebenau? the woman asked. For a long time afterwards, shame, and those waves of peculiar heat, flooded Hermine whenever she thought of it. She drank sedative teas, and bought sleeping pills.

After such bought sleep, however, the days were even harder to bear than they had been when she lay awake all night. Better a glass of beer, she told herself. Soon it was two beers and more, and to her despair of sleep was added self-disgust. She saw a doctor. An operation was advised: she had a piece of herself cut out, one she really didn't need anymore. But this organ must have been seated too far from the humor in question, for there was no improvement. On the contrary. Now her bodily powers began to desert her along with the mental. Even speech became difficult. After long hours at school she found herself too weak to get up. She sat at her desk without moving until the cleaning woman came. To tame the wild hordes—again and again she saw no way out except to give a beating, although this was strictly forbidden. Then in the nights she felt as violated by this as the children she had mishandled, and she sought the blame in herself, where she easily found it. True, some children now carried on in ways that would have been unthinkable before. She became acquainted with a new emotion: she began to hate this or that child in their midst. But it was a fickle hatred, since the worst troublemaker among them was as often as not the funniest and most likeable, as soon as Hermine had the child alone.

She had long since parted from her husband. All this rolling around, weeping, mopping at sweat, was more than she would inflict on him anymore. The dinner table was another thing, of course. All the same he often had to take a hand himself if he cared to eat anything decent. For her, the dumplings fell apart in the soup, the cake stuck to the tin and would not come out. Once when the owl cried and cried and would not leave off crying, Hermine went out on the balcony to try and see which of the little fir trees in the neighborhood it was calling from. But the cry came from off in the distance after all, from the tall trees of the not so nearby cemetery. She lay down again, and in her thoughts she followed the cry of the owl. At one grave, she could linger, the better to reproach herself all sorts of ways. And since it was so easy to travel this way, at night, to all the graveyards, she went to them ever oftener, and especially to one far away. Now, here were graves upon graves! Quite a few at which she could stand, and the accusations would pile up skyward; as high as the village church beside which the graves lay; so high they almost crushed her.

One bright autumn night—she had waited already past midnight for the owl to cry—a giant shadow flew to the railing of the balcony. "Groo-hoo," it cried, three times and no more. From that night on, Hermine knew what the owl was saying. When chaos overtook her by day, she fled ever deeper into this thought. It seemed in fact to comfort her. Some days she could scarcely think any thought but this one. When they found fault with her now, she got in the habit of thinking: "Just wait!" She only had to figure out exactly the right way to go about it, and sketched and hammered out plans in the night. On a clear night in December, the owl came again to the railing. This night she cried louder, reproachfully, as if she couldn't understand why Hermine was still there. She cried many times. Hermine counted. She thought: "If she cries thirteen times, tomorrow is the day." After the twelfth cry, she flew off. "Twelve is even more final," thought Hermine, and set the hour. At breakfast, her daughter noticed how Hermine's hand was trembling. "Last night I finally heard your owl—very creepy," she said. Whereupon her husband, too, looked at Hermine and threw down his spoon: "Now I've finally had about enough!" he shouted. From then on, she went to doctors instead of to school. Hermine should take a cure, they said. It was the first one that had ever been prescribed for her, and she expected everything of it: indeed she waited for it as full of yearning as she had looked for the Easter rabbit as a child.

Change

Birds

The cure started badly. The doctor in charge took Hermine's exact weight and measurements, then prescribed cold water, fresh air, and plenty of sleep without sleeping pills. Now the cure was already half over and nothing had changed. Same weight, same girth, since the food was nothing out of the ordinary. The fresh air was a bit too fresh: an icy, bitter wind had been blowing out of the northeast for weeks. The perambulations of all the other guests at the watering place came to an early end at a café, Hermine's most often in her lifeless room. The cold water was too cold. The dousings gave her terrible pains in her upper arms and shoulders. But worst of all was sleep. There were a lot of owls here, several different species, even. Here she had to be sleepless in the afternoons too: at least at home she had no time for that.

The afternoon rest period was half gone when, from the fir tree in front of Hermine's window, there came the cry of an owl. She leaped up in horror and saw it. It was a smaller bird, an owlet that didn't even open its beak when it screamed. Its call too was different, but if anything more insistent: *Come with, come with,* it told her very clearly. Hermine became immensely agitated. It was a sort of panic, the mood in which she scrawled a couple of sentences and fled the room as if something pursued her. In the house it was strangely quiet. Likewise out of doors, silence reigned. Only the night before, that bitter northeast wind had finally died down. Now the sky hung full of snow; here and there a solitary flake fell. There were endless forests all about this spa. Hermine walked and walked. She had always liked walking; now she wanted simply to walk away.

The deeper she went into the silent woods, the more her agitation subsided: it lapsed into a silent emptiness. After perhaps an hour, snow began to fall in earnest. It looked like Advent, although it was February. The path grew rough, then left off altogether. But she found what she was looking for: a woodpile among the bushes where she could sit as in an armchair. And still she didn't do the terrible thing that she had intended. It was too peaceful inside of her now. Besides, she was tired and suddenly falling asleep. A sound of laughter awakened her. It came from above. Was it a woodpecker or a jaybird? Trying to get a glimpse of it, she moved a little. The laughter stopped, something black flew off.

Hermine jumped to her feet and began to run back the way she had come. "You've been off your head—*unbalanced*," again and again she said that word to herself, *unbalanced*. How subtle, how on the mark, language sometimes was. Something in her was essentially out of balance—for a long time now, out of its proper place. That much she saw with great clarity. But at the same time she felt herself ready, now, to push and pull things once more to rights. Meanwhile it was snowing harder. The woods were gloomy with dusk, but the path was white. Up and down the white path ran the tracks of animals. Comings and goings—in the snow they were everywhere to be seen. Change was exchange. Creatures exchanged a less good place for a better one, or the reverse. From rest to forage, from the wide open to the secret lair. She seemed to herself to be an animal on the move, in the service of some such change. That word, *change,* took hold of her and would not let go. When it had to do with money, it was ugly and mean. And likewise when it was yoked together with life it sounded like a penance: *change of life.* She played with the word, *changeable, changeling, change one's mind,* until she felt herself going round and around. No, those were the kinds of mad changes she would not put herself through anymore! A great joy came over her, because she was still here, and now she fell hungrily on a new word, *being.* "It doesn't say *doing* or even *living.* Either of those would have been a demand. Being alone asks nothing of me," thought Hermine, and actually ran for joy.

At some fork in the path she must have run the wrong way; she had no idea which way the house lay from where she was. Meanwhile it had fallen dark in the woods. She didn't feel the slightest fear. Not even clumps of bushes and rock that looked like men had the power to frighten her. After a long time, she began to be hungry. She had read in the menu for the day that, for once, instead of turkey schnitzel, they would be having *pastete.* She'd have liked that—the local delicacy, a great sleeve of meat, halfway between a wurst and a pâté. "*Pasteten* here, *pasteten* there, *pasteten* oh! what do I care," went a children's song. She hadn't known what a *pastete* was. Maybe a cannon? So why had she never asked? Probably because she preferred not to know. There had been a lot of things that she didn't want to know, and it seemed to her, now, that she had been borne along by chance, a ship without a rudder. "That will be different from now on," she said out loud, and started at the sound of her own voice. Suddenly bells were ringing quite nearby. "Easter bells," she thought, although Christmas bells would better have suited the snowy woods. But as soon as the sound pressed at her ears, it brought back a time when, as children, they had hurried through a snowstorm to church for the Feast of the Resurrection. The weather had never much cared to fit itself to the church calendar. So how was it she had forgotten about Easter for all these years?

Then the woods came to an end. She knew at once where she was; the house was not far off. Lights were burning. She would ring the bell and say she had lost her way in the forest. But at the house door a couple were kissing. She slipped into the house beside them. They were happy to have gotten lost with such a respectable person as Hermine. Quite a few guests were still sitting around. The lost ones were the heroes of the evening, and the *pastete* was warmed up again. Hermine tore the note to bits and, in a hurry as though the terrible words might set the paper afire, flushed it away.

Hermine slept through that night, something that had not happened to her for a long time. The next morning they laughed. They kept on laughing for two full weeks. Others joined the three who wanted to laugh again as well: on the street, at house concerts, in church. It was Shrovetide. The funny lovebirds had to take their leave. Hermine was allowed to stay. The doctor saw that the countryside was doing her good. Meanwhile a great snow had fallen. Hermine walked in the woods to feed the birds. That was the best part of the cure. For the birds were quite tame there and would eat out of a person's hand. Soon there was talk about the place that the birds flocked to Hermine before any other. Some guests walked along with her especially to observe it: she was plainly favored; the shyest warblers and the boldest sparrows alike crowded to her hand. When she went to the woods alone, she wept for joy. She believed that now all would be well.

After the snow, spring charged in at full force. So Hermine had something of spring in her cure as well. This season had often made her happy. Here, in the foothills of the Alps, it had a particular charm. As they went walking across the fields, there sat a giant snowy owl in the middle of a meadow whose snow had melted here and there. There happened to be a preserve for birds of prey on one side of the spa. When performances were underway, owls from the north might be sitting on the open fields, and vultures from the south roosting in Bavarian bushes. It looked comical. Only to be funny, Hermine stretched out a hand and called: "Come, birdy." The owl looked at her with rapt attention, spread its great wings and came flying. Hermine's companions screamed. They ran away, batting their hands at it, and thus the frightened bird flew narrowly by Hermine's hand.

Then it was time for her, too, to go home. When she had packed her suitcase and sat waiting, she realized an owl was staring down at her, across the vacant dinner table, from a picture on the wall. It frightened her a little. Would it all begin again, the listening and lying awake? The longer she looked at the owl, the surer she was that it gazed at her kindly, like a friend.

Hare and Deer

Hermine was hiking once again. The woods were still a good hundred yards away. Suddenly a half-grown hare came running and crouched, trembling, at Hermine's foot. In the next moment a hawk plunged to earth close to the road. He turned a wild and angry gaze on them, then spread his giant wings and flapped off sullenly to the edge of the woods. The little hare jumped over the ditch by the side of the road, the better to hop along beside her. Only when the forest was near did he speed away.

Hermine suddenly recalled another event not unlike this one. It was a night during the bombing. The industrial city some twenty miles away was under attack. They too went to their cellar. There were rumblings, bangs, booms. The preserving jars trembled and clanked against one another. They asked themselves in horror: What are they going through now, the ones who live in the city! And on top of that, black fear crawled at the backs of their necks, for they had heard that a pilot whose bomb-release jammed while he was over his intended target would not care to fly home with this payload. So he would dump his bombs somewhere or other over their broad land. Hermine couldn't stand it any longer in the cellar. Besides, she needed to see for herself what such a night would look like.

When she opened the front door, a strange sight indeed

awaited her. Close to the door, with their heads turned to it and so, now, facing Hermine in the open doorway, stood a herd of deer; on the outer edge of the herd were three bucks. The sky, from the south, flickered fiery red. And likewise the eyes of the deer, so deep with fear, lit up red. Now Hermine had a mute conversation with them. "You are off your heads," she told them, "your healthier instincts have abandoned you. You are seeking protection from humans, in their human habitations. But there is nothing in the world so wicked as humankind. At any other time, you know that yourselves." She would have had more to say to them. But now someone else couldn't endure it any longer in the cellar, or likewise had to have a look-around to see if the world was still there. At the sight of the deer, this person cried out in astonishment. That frightened them, but not so that they ran wildly away; rather, they all, in the same moment, turned in their tracks. As if disappointed, they walked slowly out of the farmyard. Only once they had gotten a certain distance away, they began, after the manner of deer, to run for the woods.

Frog

In the paper, Hermine read about a part of the country where she had liked to go walking years ago. Because there was a wetland in the place, it had been declared a nature preserve. "I'd like to go there sometime soon," Hermine coaxed. By chance she ran into a fellow teacher from her former school. "Are you up to hiking again?" the woman asked. And Hermine told her about her latest fancy. Then the teacher wanted to come along—and she would bring her husband. On the spot, they set a date and time. It was a long drive to get there. Hardly worth it for a waterhole in a swamp, the two husbands were thinking; you could see it in their sullen faces.

An old man standing by the chart of raptor birds growled: "No use coming here nowadays—you'll see nary a frog." The men walked in front and talked politics. The former colleague told tales about the school, or rather about the other teachers. Hermine was happy to hear something of them again. "This one dresses as crazy as ever, that one is sick more often than she's in school—she should have quit long ago, another one's husband is rolling in it—she doesn't need to be taking the bread out of the young ones' mouths." Hermine was on the point of regretting that they had driven this long way when the former colleague went on: "This one and that one are still having their affair. You have to feel sorry for the wife. But nobody knows for absolutely certain, because they're very careful." In this case, however, Hermine knew for absolutely certain. She was proud to be able to offer this certainty to the injured husband. "I know—" "Quark, quark, quark," came a croaking quite nearby. "Psst," said Hermine, and saw him. He was a magnificent fellow, a puffed-up, mottled frog. And careful—for now he held his peace. Hermine stood still, watched and waited. This went on too long for the former colleague. She joined the men, since about politics she also knew a thing or two.

Then the frog began to croak once more. Other frogs answered him. And now Hermine heard how quiet it was in the marshland. It gurgled, chirped, hummed. She heard birdcalls that were completely new to her. The raptor bird that she had seen on the poster at the entrance cast down its cry from the air. And what she saw! On the pond was a mother duck with so many ducklings—more than you could count. What Hermine took, at first, for a branch turned out to be a heron, once she came close. She saw dragonflies and beetles of all sorts. Now plants too began to show themselves to her, among them some that she hadn't seen for years, and that made her actually tremble. She walked slowly, quietly. Often she didn't walk at all. A great happiness overtook her, that all this was still here. She caught, with care, a charming little tree frog, to show it to those who waited for her impatiently. They too should get to see some small thing from the glorious marsh. As she reached her party, a stork swept by, over their heads, on its way into the swamp. "Just leave my big frog in peace," Hermine called out to him. "Your wife seems to like frogs," the former colleague said to Hermine's husband. He turned to Hermine and stroked her cheek tenderly with the back of his hand.

Marten

One rainy Sunday, some relations, a young married couple, came to visit. They had brought their two children along. The boy wanted to go straight out into the yard. But the wet weather had made a morass of Hermine's garden. She feared for her parlor floor in its Sunday brightest, and so forbid Alexander the garden. He raged and screamed. His parents, who had not sat down yet, were half embarrassed, half offended that their child should not have his wish fulfilled. Still shaking with fury, Alexander sat down in the armchair at the window. "What does that animal want from me?" he said.

Now they all looked at the window. On the wide window ledge a marten was standing. It stood, in fact, upright, showing its handsome white breast and sharp teeth. As it leaned there so calmly, it broadcast about it the sense of threat that dead, stuffed animals do. They all gazed at it spellbound.

Hermine was acquainted with the marten; she lived across the way in an old shed. A square hole in the gable on top of the shed roof was her door and window. Hermine often had to wipe away the paw prints from her own windowpane in the morning: the marten was given to hunting for spiders and beetles at night along the warm glass. From inside the trance that held them all, someone said, "Well, even so, martens belong in the woods."

And, that quickly, the creature was gone. Alexander's mother comforted her son: "It didn't want anything from you," but Hermine said: "She wanted to see who had come to visit." "Why doesn't she stay in the woods?" the boy asked peevishly.

Hermine explained. "Well, for her it's a matter of life and death. Because of the poisons we've sprayed along the lakeshore, lots of birds have died. But martens live on birds' eggs, and baby birds too. So their hunting grounds have had to get larger and larger. This marten was probably chased out by a stronger one. That's why she moved to the middle of the city. And it suits her. She looks for food in gardens and trashcans. She fetches leftover bits of sandwiches from the schoolyards at night. She even nibbles car tires. She's been living here three years already. Early in the morning I often watch her four young ones playing on the roof." "But there are only three," said Alexander. Sure enough, three charming baby martens were chasing each other on the rooftop. They watched them, how they stood up high on their haunches like little men. Suddenly the old marten leaped onto the roof with prey in her mouth. The three little martens disappeared in a flash. "A rat," somebody said. The big marten set her catch free, and they saw that it was her fourth young one. She bit the little one, and it screamed. Marten shrieks are ugly. But the young marten didn't run away; cowering and snarling, it let itself be thrashed. All the way to the hole in the gable, it took its beating. No one needed to point out that this was punishment for disobedience.

All the same Hermine said: "The highway is right over there. And the man in the second house down has bought himself a rifle on account of the martens." "You mean their mama won't let them run and play?" the little girl asked. "She has to rest during the day, because at night she has to look for food," said Hermine. "What about the papa?" "There is no papa, you dumb—" But then Alexander took a lesson from the marten.

They never really settled down to a visit. With the animals so close by, no one was quite in the mood. They had parked their car even nearer to the martens' hole. "I hope they see her," thought Hermine, for the marten was peering out like a know-it-all neighbor, always on the lookout for right and wrong. "Like woman, like marten," Hermine said to herself, and felt the goose pimples rise on her arms.

Blackbird

Once, in bright midday, Hermine had a dream. She was back home, standing in a place where no one ever liked to stand. It was more a hiding place than a place, but no one used it when they played hide-and-seek. Only when you were hiding from some punishment would you go there, or when you were ashamed. It was the corner of the barn where the whim-gin was built on, angled to the north, where no sun ever came. Because of that, the roof tiles of the shed were always damp and slick with moss. Its wall boards were black and rotting away. One board had been missing since time was; that was where you could slip through to hide. The bull's paddock, where the cows were bred, was in this desolate corner. Consequently the place had a sinful air about it. Moreover from the barn floor a tile stuck out that drained, in a narrow trickle, a stinking brew from the dung puddle into the berry garden. In her dream, Hermine was indeed trying to slip into the hole. She knew herself to be in deep disgrace.

Then one of her dead brothers passed by, offhandedly, not for her sake, but he looked at her all the same. She wanted to ask him how it was that everything had gone so wrong, but before she could open her mouth, he called to her, just as they used to chant it to each other as children: "It's your own fault, serves you right." She understood, from those words, everything that he was thinking, and that he had said it to her, as one must, in order to get around the horned behemoth, the furry, hairy, spiny one with the tail who loomed in the way. She wanted to cry out to him that he had had it easy, he had been able to leap over all of it, while he was still young, with his immortal soul. But he wasn't looking at her any longer. Instead he aimed the stick that he was carrying at the edge of the ditch and jumped, like a pole-vaulter, much too high and too far over the stinking rivulet. Just as Hermine was watching this jump-gone-wrong, another of her brothers was there, one who had fallen in the war. But he was already going away, over his shoulder one of the scythes that hung there on the barn wall. He looked back—looked at her, Hermine, with compassion, or so it seemed to her.

He had once been the one she trusted most. She wanted to run after him. She wanted to ask him whether everything was really so bad; what mattered; how was it afterwards? But as soon as he saw these impertinent questions on the way, he went faster and started to whistle. He was a good whistler. It was more like singing than whistling—Hermine had never heard anyone whistle so beautifully. Suddenly she wasn't standing anymore in the desolate place, but on that little rise behind the house from which one could see far into the fields and meadows. Her spirits were no longer heavy-laden: she was happy. And there went her brother with the scythe, ever farther down the track into the fields. The farther he went, the louder and gladder he whistled. Just as she began to wonder at this, she woke up. It was a blackbird singing outside her window.

photo by Roman Pichler

Maria Beig was born in rural Upper Swabia, in the south of Germany, in 1920. Author of eight novels and four short story collections, she won the Alemannischer Literaturpreis in 1983, the Literaturpreis of the City of Stuttgart in 1997, and the Hebel-Preis in 2004.

New Issues Poetry & Prose

Editor, Herbert Scott

Vito Aiuto, *Self-Portrait as Jerry Quarry*
James Armstrong, *Monument In A Summer Hat*
Claire Bateman, *Clumsy*
Maria Beig, *Hermine: An Animal Life* (fiction)
Michael Burkard, *Pennsylvania Collection Agency*
Christopher Bursk, *Ovid at Fifteen*
Anthony Butts, *Fifth Season*
Anthony Butts, *Little Low Heaven*
Kevin Cantwell, *Something Black in the Green Part of Your Eye*
Gladys Cardiff, *A Bare Unpainted Table*
Kevin Clark, *In the Evening of No Warning*
Cynie Cory, *American Girl*
Jim Daniels, *Night with Drive-By Shooting Stars*
Joseph Featherstone, *Brace's Cove*
Lisa Fishman, *The Deep Heart's Core Is a Suitcase*
Robert Grunst, *The Smallest Bird in North America*
Paul Guest, *The Resurrection of the Body and the Ruin of the World*
Robert Haight, *Emergences and Spinner Falls*
Mark Halperin, *Time as Distance*
Myronn Hardy, *Approaching the Center*
Brian Henry, *Graft*
Edward Haworth Hoeppner, *Rain Through High Windows*
Cynthia Hogue, *Flux*
Christine Hume, *Alaskaphrenia*
Janet Kauffman, *Rot* (fiction)
Josie Kearns, *New Numbers*
Maurice Kilwein Guevara, *Autobiography of So-and-so: Poems in Prose*
Ruth Ellen Kocher, *When the Moon Knows You're Wandering*
Ruth Ellen Kocher, *One Girl Babylon*
Gerry LaFemina, *Window Facing Winter*

Steve Langan, *Freezing*
Lance Larsen, *Erasable Walls*
David Dodd Lee, *Abrupt Rural*
David Dodd Lee, *Downsides of Fish Culture*
M.L. Liebler, *The Moon a Box*
Deanne Lundin, *The Ginseng Hunter's Notebook*
Barbara Maloutas, *In a Combination of Practices*
Joy Manesiotis, *They Sing to Her Bones*
Sarah Mangold, *Household Mechanics*
Gail Martin, *The Hourglass Heart*
David Marlatt, *A Hog Slaughtering Woman*
Louise Mathias, *Lark Apprentice*
Gretchen Mattox, *Buddha Box*
Gretchen Mattox, *Goodnight Architecture*
Paula McLain, *Less of Her*
Sarah Messer, *Bandit Letters*
Malena Mörling, *Ocean Avenue*
Julie Moulds, *The Woman with a Cubed Head*
Gerald Murnane, *The Plains* (fiction)
Marsha de la O, *Black Hope*
C. Mikal Oness, *Water Becomes Bone*
Bradley Paul, *The Obvious*
Elizabeth Powell, *The Republic of Self*
Margaret Rabb, *Granite Dives*
Rebecca Reynolds, *The Bovine Two-Step*
Rebecca Reynolds, *Daughter of the Hangnail*
Martha Rhodes, *Perfect Disappearance*
Beth Roberts, *Brief Moral History in Blue*
John Rybicki, *Traveling at High Speeds* (expanded second edition)
Mary Ann Samyn, *Inside the Yellow Dress*
Mary Ann Samyn, *Purr*
Ever Saskya, *The Porch is a Journey Different From the House*
Mark Scott, *Tactile Values*
Martha Serpas, *Côte Blanche*
Diane Seuss-Brakeman, *It Blows You Hollow*
Elaine Sexton, *Sleuth*

Marc Sheehan, *Greatest Hits*
Sarah Jane Smith, *No Thanks—and Other Stories* (fiction)
Heidi Lynn Staples, *Guess Can Gallop*
Phillip Sterling, *Mutual Shores*
Angela Sorby, *Distance Learning*
Matthew Thorburn, *Subject to Change*
Russell Thorburn, *Approximate Desire*
Rodney Torreson, *A Breathable Light*
Robert VanderMolen, *Breath*
Martin Walls, *Small Human Detail in Care of National Trust*
Patricia Jabbeh Wesley, *Before the Palm Could Bloom: Poems of Africa*